JANAKA AND ASHTAVAKRA

Ashraf Karayath was born in Nadapuram, a village in Kerala, India. After finishing his MA in English Literature, he migrated to Dubai in 1991. He has twenty-five years of business experience coupled with a background in management philosophy. Despite his professional preoccupations, he continues in his quest to unravel the timeless knowledge of ancient Indian culture.

Winner of **PVLF Author Excellence Award**, organized by the Federation of Indian Publishers, Frontlist Media and Nielsen India.

'Unlike regular mythology novels, Ashraf Karayath's recent work *Janaka and Ashtavakra* proves that a mythological story is not only something with which we can pride our cultural heritage, but also about philosophical and spiritual insights that are beyond borders, religion, politics and everything that divides humanity.'
—*The Times of India*

'Ashraf Karayath's *Janaka and Ashtavakra: A Journey Beyond* proves that mythology may not be just something of the past; these tales draw parallels to our present stories.'
—*The Week*, largest circulated news magazine in India

'As the world grapples with the COVID-19 pandemic, Ashraf Karayath's debut novel *Janaka and Ashtavakra: A Journey Beyond*, published by Rupa Publications, sets a new meaning of life.'
—*The New Indian Express*

'While most of the mythological creations show the winning of good over evil, Ashraf's novel lucidly deciphers more about the endearing spirit that makes our lives worthy of everything.'
—*The Morning Standard*

'The seeds of the book grew out of the author's knowledge he gained in the hustle and bustle of Dubai's business world.'
—*Mathrubumi*, leading news daily newspaper

'The mythological novel answers some of the questions pertaining to the absolute realities of life.'
—*The Hitavada*, largest selling English daily newspaper in central India

'*Janaka and Ashtavakra* [...] is already soon rising to be the top 20 bestsellers on Amazon.'

—*Gulf News*, UAE

'This book makes spirituality the main essence, and this is mingled with the basic story in such a way that even beginners and people not inclined to spirituality can connect with it very well.'

—*Dailyhunt*

'Contextualizing a mythological tale, the book strives into the questions of the ultimate realities of life in the modern world.'

—*Doha News*, Qatar

Reader Reviews

'It changed my life... Opened doors for me. "I read a book one day and my whole life was changed," says Orhan Pamuk in his famous book, *The New Life*. I am experiencing it now. This morning, I completed reading Ashraf Karayath's novel, *Janaka and Ashtavakra: A Journey Beyond*, and I am changed.'

—**Suresh Shekharan**,
Blogger and Writer

'Fascinating insight into one of the most significant dialogue in spiritual history. If I had to rate it amongst the books I have read in the genre of Indian mysticism, I would rate this in the top two. The book is un-put-downable. It deserves to be read and experienced by many, many people.'

—**Rugmani Prabhakar**,
AOL Teacher, Bangalore, India

'One of the best books I have ever read. I started reading, thinking it was like any other spiritual book on the same lines as *Ashtavakra*

Gita, which is a popular scripture on self-realization. However, I was pleasantly surprised to see that this book brought out a totally different dimension about King Janaka and Mithila.'

—**Vijay Kumar Kunnath**

'Very well written book. As a young entrepreneur myself, this is a great book for me to read especially in the genre of fiction as it beautifully guides the mental state of Janaka balancing his duties as a king, father, husband and his spiritual journey. I urge everyone to read *'Janaka and Ashtavakra'* as it's the perfect ingredient in today's chaotic and very transactional recipe of life to bring a wholesome goodness.'

—**Shivanath Devinarayanan**, CEO, Dazeworks

'Beautifully conveyed through a story told in uncomplicated prose. Ashraf's book is a motivational guide with a deeply positive message for today's uncertain times.'

—**Madhavi Murthy**, Dubai

JANAKA AND ASHTAVAKRA

A Journey Beyond

Ashraf Karayath

RUPA

Published by
Rupa Publications India Pvt. Ltd 2020
7/16, Ansari Road, Daryaganj
New Delhi 110002

Sales centres:
Bengaluru Chennai
Hyderabad Jaipur Kathmandu
Kolkata Mumbai Prayagraj

Copyright © Ashraf Karayath 2020

This is a work of fiction. Names, characters, places and incidents are either the product of the author's imagination or are used fictitiously and any resemblance to any actual person, living or dead, events or locales is entirely coincidental.

All rights reserved.
No part of this publication may be reproduced, transmitted, or stored in a retrieval system, in any form or by any means, electronic, mechanical, photocopying, recording or otherwise, without the prior permission of the publisher.

P-ISBN: 978-93-89967-05-0
E-ISBN: 978-93-89967-06-7

Eleventh impression 2025

20 19 18 17 16 15 14 13 12 11

The moral right of the author has been asserted.

Printed in India

This book is sold subject to the condition that it shall not, by way of trade or otherwise, be lent, resold, hired out, or otherwise circulated, without the publisher's prior consent, in any form of binding or cover other than that in which it is published.

'Wake up from your sleep and start walking. You are blissfully immersed with the slumber of self-ignorance. You are only a dream walker in this world of illusions (mithya), an ever-changing appearance of maya. Wake up from your dream and do what needs to be done to gain the ability to see yourself as you really are.'

Kathopanishad

Contents

Prologue   *xi*

BOOK ONE: MITHYA

The King	3
The Young Sage	5
The King's Brother	13
Predictions	26
The Wise Minister	34
Sita	41
Uddalaka's Revelation and Mahosadha's Predicament	48
The Secret	55
Ahimsa	59

BOOK TWO: SAMSARA

The King's Confidante	69
Preparations	76
Swayamvar	83
The Arrogant King	92
The Queen's Plight	97
Whispers in the Night	105

BOOK THREE: SANKALPA

The Prisoner	113
The Arrival	120

Kushadwaja Asserts Himself	129
The Forest	135
The Bow in the Hall	145
Kushadwaja's Escape	152

BOOK FOUR: MAYA

Wild Rumours	159
Seeking Liberation	164
The World We Create	169
The Rope and the Snake	176
The Conflict	180
Confession	186
The Seed and the Plant	192
Fear	198
The Veil	203
Illusions	208
Epilogue	213

Prologue

The end, when it came, was sudden. Too sudden. Janaka Maharaj, the legendary king of Mithila, was captured. He knew that all empires, however wisely ruled, come to an end. And invariably, that end would be as quick and decisive as the swinging of a sword above a kneeling man's head.

Surrounded by rebels and the mutilated bodies of his trusted private guards, fear crept into King Janaka's bones as sharp steel was levelled against his throat. Dropping his sword and falling to his knees, he waited, utterly trapped and alone, for the final blow.

The walls around him vibrated as the palace horses outside, pounded the dusty ground with their hooves. Elephant shrieks pierced the air and added to the chilling clamour of clashing swords, and the tortured screams of men. An enraged crowd swarmed the palace. Arrows smashed windows and hammers clanged against the statues of heroes from Mithila's past. Sculptures, passed down through generations, fell to the ground and shattered. The heads of the kingdom's defenders fell, as blood spurted across the royal wall, spattering paintings and tapestries. Panic-stricken women gathering stray children were swept along hopelessly in the tide of violence.

To the king's horror, the rampaging mob set fire to his majestic palace before his very eyes. The growing inferno mercilessly lit the gilded throne, illuminating the brightly painted ceilings. The blaze moved on to feed upon intricately carved balconies, where the ladies of the palace once idled away countless hours, watching the happenings in the courtyard below. Finally, the rising flames reflected on the ivory marble floor, transformed into the colours of a dying sunset. Dark clouds of smoke billowed into the sky and spread across the city, carrying into the blackening horizon, the ghosts of everyone the once-great and invincible ruler had known and loved.

❊

The once regal face of the great king, Janaka Maharaj, was now clouded with bewilderment; he had been disarmed and blind folded. His hands were tied and he was tossed like a sack of grain upon a hard saddle, his crown falling to the ground. The horse's heaving sides and its trembling body revealed the animal's fear. It lurched away as soon as it was set free, desperately racing across plains, forests and mountains. Finally, it slowly collapsed in exhaustion at the base of a gnarled tree.

The king lay still upon the horse, broken and exhausted. The stench of the beast filled his nostrils. Every inch of his body was bruised from the harsh journey. Pain seized him as he rolled off and collapsed to the ground. He saw that he was on a dirt path outside a humble village on the outskirts of his former kingdom. Dazed, Janaka stumbled to his feet. He glimpsed rows of low mud huts. Their doors were so small that it was difficult for him to imagine a human being able to enter through them. The smell of animal dung soured the breeze. Janaka's nostrils rebelled against it.

Half-naked children playing in the dust stopped their games to gaze at him. The villagers in the streets, eyes wide with surprise, took in the sight of the ghostly figure. Nobody recognized him and he lacked the courage to announce that he had once been their king. His palace, his courtiers, the pomp and luxury that had once accompanied his status: everything of that life now hovered ghostlike, a distant dream.

Janaka recognized nothing. Exhausted and in need of food and water, he wandered towards the dusty streets, stooping like an old man. He tried to walk towards one of the huts, but lost his balance and crumpled to the ground. He lay there until he regained some strength. He stood up again, slowly this time, and looked at his torn and shabby clothes. His feet were bare, his ornaments and gold earrings were gone. His mud-caked hands weakly swatted at the flies buzzing around his head.

He had no place to rest. No food. Hunger pangs made him want to cry out. Anything would suffice, even a piece of bread, a bowl of porridge, some rice soup. He needed something to fill the gnawing hole in his stomach.

He saw a man holding a piece of bread, tearing off pieces from it and stuffing them into his mouth. Janaka approached the man slowly. 'Please,' he choked out despite the thick coating of sand in his throat, 'I beg of you. Could you spare some of your food?'

But the man's features grew tight with anger. 'Be gone with you,' he barked, waving his hand and shooing Janaka away.

Janaka stumbled forward. The gnawing in his stomach was growing more insistent. This time, he approached one of the huts and knocked weakly. A woman opened the door. Her lips pursed immediately with suspicion and fear. 'Please,' he whispered. But before he could finish begging, the whoosh of the door closing in his face knocked him back a step. It was the same with everyone. Wherever he went, he was turned away. The people he asked looked at one another, fear and anxiety etched on their faces. Door after door closed.

After wandering some time in the dust and sun, he reached a temple. People were waiting in a queue. He joined the line of men and women of all shapes and sizes. There were children too, dressed in tattered rags, their faces and hair matted with dirt. The queue moved slowly, until finally, he reached the end where food was being served. There, Janaka was neither a king nor a commoner. He was just a beggar, waiting for his turn. Soon, he was standing before a bony fellow who stank of stale sweat and ignored him and his outstretched hands. A beggar standing by took pity on him and pointed silently towards a nearby banana tree.

Janaka understood. He plucked a long leaf, folding it into a bowl. Cupping its greenness in both hands, he reached out to receive his meagre portion of the bland gruel. It was hot. Janaka flinched and spilled some of it on his bare leg. The man stared and shooed him away.

Janaka hobbled over to the shade of a tree and sat down. The food smelled foul, but it was all he had. He would devour it like it was the first course of a banquet.

However, no sooner had he raised the bowl to his lips, two great dogs charged by chasing one another. They knocked off the leaf and the food it contained from his hands. The gruel disappeared into the dirt. Then, just as he thought things could not get any worse, he heard a hideous cackling behind him. Looking around, he saw an old woman doubled with age, staring at him and laughing maniacally. She had only one good eye. The other was white and lifeless, but it still peered into his soul as if she had known him all her life.

Stunned, Janaka looked into her dead white eye. A series of images started to play out, as if projected on its milky white screen. He saw flames and murder, betrayal and death; loved ones perishing as his empire fell, all in vivid, excruciating detail. He tried to turn away, but a shrivelled old hand pulled him back.

'These things you keep, they will be taken from you. See what you have wrought... Do you know now if you are a beggar or a king?'

BOOK ONE
MITHYA

You are what you think.
If you think you are bound, you are bound.
If you think you are free, you are free.

1.11 ASHTAVAKRA GITA

The King

Surrounded by his courtiers, ministers and relatives, the horror-stricken king jolted upright in the seat of his throne. Beautiful young girls on either side bent their questioning faces towards him as they waved their colourful feather fans gently. A breeze rich with sandalwood touched his dream-clouded face. All his courtiers had been standing by in silence, waiting for him to awaken from his deep slumber.

Janaka stared in disbelief at what he saw around him, his commanding visage with its flowing grey beard and hair, eclipsed only slightly by the dark shadow of the dream. He remembered it vividly. But surely it was a dream! Surely he was now awake?

As if to prove to himself what he had just experienced was nothing but a bad dream, he dropped his hands on his lap and touched his thighs. Yes! His rich garments were still there, he could feel the seed pearls and gold between his fingers. Then his hands moved up tentatively to feel his golden crown. All there... as they should be. He was King Janaka, the ruler of Mithila.

But he was still not reassured. He needed to cast his eyes upon his palace. He looked at the hall with its royal gilded dais, with its pillars carved from white marble and etched with images of gods and goddesses, its giant doors embossed with beaten metals, the silver threads of its yellow curtains sparkling in the sunlight and paintings of former kings hanging in their places.

These sights brought only momentary relief. Terror suddenly gripped him as he looked around once more, wondering if he had spoken in his sleep and if anyone had noticed something was amiss. He was fully awake now, but the effect of the dream was such that the familiar surroundings felt alien. In the gaping space that appeared in his mind, the dream had pushed him into a new place that was equally confusing and mystifying.

He felt afresh the wounds inflicted during the dream. His hands throbbed, and the place where the hot gruel had scalded his leg still burned. But there were no marks. He shook his head a few times, hoping to rattle his consciousness back into place. The courtiers looked at him in mute question. They would wait, he knew, until their king sought to share his thoughts with them.

But Janaka was unsure. He felt that something significant had happened. He was changed somehow. And a question nagged at him. What if it had not been a dream? What if it had been much more? To Janaka, if what he had seen in the dream was the truth, then it followed that what he was looking at now, his present palace and courtiers, could only be shadows.

He sat up, narrowed his eyes, and searched the hall one last time.

Which one is real?
Who am I?
A beggar or a king?

The Young Sage

The still evening deepened to darkness. All was quiet around the little thatched hut. Sujata lay awake, lost in her thoughts, remembering the day's events. Ever since her son, Ashtavakra, left for the ashram two days earlier, she had been biding her time, keeping herself occupied with small things. The emptiness of the house seemed to weigh more heavily with every passing hour. For fourteen years, it had been just her and her son. She had asked Ashtavakra many times not to move to a gurukul at such an early age. Young as he was, he had proved himself wise beyond his years, but his deformed body limited him. After many futile attempts at pleading and reasoning with him, she finally let her only child leave her protective embrace. Until the day he returned from the gurukul, Sujata decided that she would keep herself busy and not brood over his absence.

She turned to look in surprise as the door opened wide and a crooked figure entered without a word, deepening the silence of the night. With his rolling, uneven gait, Ashtavakra staggered towards his mother, barefoot. Except for the coarse white dhoti covering his loins, he was not clothed. A dark-beaded necklace, a Rudraksh mala, hung around his neck while another dangled loosely around his right wrist, leaving his body exposed and vulnerable. He bent his bald head to look at Sujata, his dark, deep-set eyes fixed on her. She got up and made as if to welcome him. But before Sujata could say a word, Ashtavakra took another step towards her. His right leg was wrapped around his walking stick, like a vine hugging the trunk of a mighty tree. His misshapen and crooked spine had forced him to lean heavily on this wooden cane. Shrivelled skin pulled and stretched over his twisted limbs that protruded at odd angles. He clutched a dusty jute bag. The lines in his skin came together, forming deep crevices on his gaunt face as he squinted at Sujata.

She was bewildered. 'Why have you returned so early?'

Silence prevailed for some time. The only prominent noise was the boy's ragged breathing. Without a word, he hung the jute bag on a wooden peg protruding from the wall, turned to her and said, 'Mother!'

Sujata was startled by the intensity of his voice. His face was calm, but the embers in his eyes stirred up within her a feeling of uncontrollable dread. Her child had never addressed her this way before.

'Who is my father?' he asked, gently but firmly.

Her lips parted. A chill grew in her chest. It spread to the rest of her worn body just as night spreads over the earth.

Sujata remained still, unable to speak. Knowing him, she knew he would not go back without an answer. As she struggled to find her courage, silence echoed between the walls of their tiny abode.

'Mother! Many times I have asked this question and many times you have been unable to answer. But now, please, I must know.'

As the silence deepened, his face became aflame with determination. But from the depth of his resolve, a wave of strength emerged, animating his frail form.

'Did anything happen, Ashtavakra?' his mother asked

weakly, to distract him.

'I am asking you again, Mother. Who is my real father?' He must know the answer. Years of unending curiosity and emotions had made the weight of this question too large a burden for him to bear. His mother had always deflected his questions, artfully leading the conversation to a different subject.

'Why do you keep asking this question repeatedly?' she asked him, pretending not to be shocked. 'Sage Uddalaka is your father.'

'There is no one who deserves the title more. I know that. In my heart, Uddalaka is like my father, but he is not. I love my grandfather dearly, but I need to know.' He looked at her pleadingly, 'I need to know who my father is!'

Long gone were the days when it was easy for her to console him. When Ashtavakra was a child, Sujata's younger brother, Swetaketu, had given the young boy a glimpse of the truth. Ashtavakra was sitting on Uddalaka's lap when Swetaketu's jealousy took over him. He demanded that Ashtavakra get down. 'You go and sit on your father's lap. This is my father.'

Since then, Ashtavakra had burned to know the truth.

She could no longer find a way to escape the boy's questions.

Sujata looked at the frail, disfigured body of her beloved son and exhaled. She hadn't realized how much he had grown. His inner strength, his sense of worth, radiated from his wide forehead, and his ardent will and fiery thoughts sharpened his visage. His mind was voracious. He had devoured the teachings of the Vedas and the Upanishads and was constantly in discussions with elderly yogis. He had been invited by the nearby ashram, a magnificent centre of spiritual debate, where astute intellects warred over premises, assumptions, hypotheses and conclusions on the subject of Truth. The child, who had crawled on his feeble, curved legs, overcame these difficulties. Armed with the strength of the Vedas' timeless and universal knowledge, he could adopt any philosophical position and had become so brilliant at it that he could convince all his adherents to convert to any opposing philosophy.

'Why do you still think of me as a child? How ignorant do you think I am? Did you believe that I would not know the difference between my grandfather and a father?' Ashtavakra's voice trembled as he spoke. 'I need an answer.' His voice rose slightly. 'I have waited long enough. Tell me now. Who is my father?' His posture was strong, and he stood steadfast, like a banyan tree. A worry passed through her heart, and she realized that nothing in the world could move him from his need to know.

She answered with her head bowed, afraid to look at the young man. 'Ask your grandfather, and he will tell you.'

'Why should I have to ask someone else? This is between the two of us. Is it not my birthright? Will you keep even that from me?'

Sujata struggled to keep her calm. She took hold of the tip of her sari pallu and wiped the sweat forming at her brows and temples. She let out a sigh, a sigh expressing her deepest fears from having kept a secret for fourteen years. She closed her eyes.

As he stepped closer to her, his heart warmed at the sight of his mother's quivering body. He placed his hand on her shoulder and waited for the revelation to pass through her trembling lips. He felt compassion for his mother's anxiety. She looked at him, silently begging that he let go of the matter.

Ashtavakra took a deep breath and spoke in a calm, low voice. 'Mother, I am ready,' he said simply, and continued. 'I have emerged victorious from the hardship that this body has inflicted on me, successful over the challenges that the yogis have set before me. I am ready for this truth.'

'I will tell you everything, my dear son. Everything,' she sighed, closing her eyes.

When she began, her voice was soft and hesitant. 'Your father was Sage Kahoda, a disciple of Sage Uddalaka, your grandfather.'

Having now for the first time heard his father's name, Ashtavakra lowered himself slowly on the mat in front of his mother. He leaned his back on the wall and looked up at Sujata silently.

'Your grandfather, Uddalaka, was a great sage, and his glory was known across the land. Many young men came here to the ashram to seek him as their guru. One of them was your father, Kahoda. He was brilliant and handsome and from the moment he first set eyes on me, I knew my life would be empty if he was not to be a part of it.' Sujata paused. There was a tenderness in her voice, but also a sense of relief that she, at last, was able to relay to her beloved son that which she had kept secret for so long.

'And Uddalaka was so pleased with him that he offered him my hand in marriage.'

Ashtavakra's eyes widened, hungering for more.

She observed the warmth of Ashtavakra's eyes, which remained as calm and inviting as Kahoda's had been on the night they met so long ago. In the silence, with her son's eyes still upon her, Sujata felt her heart melting, and she continued.

'The nights were deep, as the lamps bathed everything

in their golden glow. We talked together—softly, sweetly, secretly—falling deeper and deeper into silence, into the unity of our being. Then, before we knew it, dawn was blushing. And when we were separated from each other, even for a day or a week, our hearts were gone, our sleep and minds departed, our bodies merely existing. Each twilight, each night and each dawn of separation seemed like a thousand years.'

A brief silence followed. Then Sujatha said softly, 'We were poor. What will love and poverty not make a man do? A poor man's wife becomes a genius at doling out food in small portions. She sleeps on a bed of straw. A poor man's mind has no use, but for his daydreams. His children, in tattered clothes, wander over to neighbours' houses, loitering about their doorways and casting hungry glances at those eating. Knowing that without action a brilliant intellect is only a burden, Kahoda went searching for a way to make a good living so that we could become comfortable, and more importantly, prove that his knowledge and intellect could bear fruit.' She paused mournfully. 'But he never returned.'

Silence reigned for some time. Tears flowed from her eyes as long-submerged emotions surged back toward the surface of her heart.

'I waited for a long time for him to come back, but he never did. I searched endlessly, but found no sign of him. In the end, I was left with no choice but to go back to my father, Sage Uddalaka. I have been here ever since. This is the truth, my son.'

Sujata hesitated to continue. Now that Ashtavakra knew some part of the truth, his soul would be frantic until he found out the full truth. If that happened, if her dear son set out on such an impossible quest, he might never return to her, just like his father.

'Many years later, I heard that Kahoda lost a debate to King Janaka's scholar saint, Bandi, who rips apart the arguments of his opponents like a vulture ripping apart a piece of meat thrown into the air. Nobody though, can question a king about the plight of those who fail in court debates. Some people say that your father challenged Bandi, who accepted under one condition: that whoever lost must pay with his life.'

Ashtavakra took hold of his stick, balanced himself as he rose up from the mat, and grabbed his jute bag from the wall.

'Ashtavakra, what are you doing?'

Without looking at her, he replied, 'I am going to discover what really happened. I need to know. If my father was last seen at the palace, then the king must know.'

Sujata quickly rose to her feet. 'You cannot go to the king just like that. You don't have a reason to go to the palace. The guards will stop you from entering. They could throw you in prison!'

'So what?' he asked, surprising his mother. 'I have every reason to go to this king's palace. No one can stop me from finding the truth.'

'No, please don't, Ashta. I don't want to lose you as well,' wailed Sujata. She couldn't hold back her tears as she thought of the pain of losing her only child, her precious Ashta.

She had only one choice left.

'Then we shall talk to your grandfather first.' Sujata said, hoping that Uddalaka would hold him back.

Ashtavakra paused for a while, as if he had arrived at a certain point, then turned and left. But just as he took his first few faltering steps, he was struck by a vision. Vividly, he saw himself at the gate of a glittering palace, being refused entry by a heavily armed guard. Then in the most powerful part of the vision, he saw a king holding a set of scales. On one scale there was life, on the other, death. And there was the king, kneeling in front of someone. Someone young...and with a twisted frame. The king was kneeling in front of him...

The King's Brother

King Janaka woke up during *Brahma Muhurta*, when the universe is in its natural stillness before the inevitable intervention of dawn. It was an ideal time to engage in contemplation, with no interference from the waking world. Janaka hardly ever missed *Brahma Muhurta*, a time when trees, plants and animals were restfully awake, poised in the boundless stillness before starting the new day.

Janaka usually woke up at this hour to meditate and then contemplate the day ahead. It was a deliberate and reflective start that helped anchor him in stillness through the day. He took in a deep breath to calm his mind and began his meditation. But calm would not come to him today. Something was bothering him—a sense of foreboding was creeping into his mind. The minute he shut his eyes, he felt himself being carried across a barren land, tied to a galloping horse, the cackling of the witch echoing against the landscape. The ghost of a thick, coarse rope cutting painfully into his skin compelled him to rub his wrists to make sure he was truly free. His skin felt smooth against his fingertips, and relief washed over him. He reached out to touch his crown that lay on a silken cushion on an ornate table beside his bed. He felt reassured, but even as he touched the symbol of his leadership, his arms trembled.

Is the dream revealing another facet of my life? One I have never seen before or experienced? What if this is what my future holds?

Must I become a beggar? Scraping for morsels? Or perhaps the dream is telling me that I am already a beggar?

The sound of the morning drums heralding the change of the guards brought Janaka out of his reverie however, his usual calm, his commanding glance and his overflowing sense of benign authority eluded him this morning. Yet duty beckoned. He gave up trying to concentrate or reason, feeling instead, deep within himself, a growing awareness that he was at the height of a great spiritual awakening. Much like the lotus flower, he knew that the soul could truly blossom only after enduring the toil of struggle and torment.

※

Kushadwaja hurried the whole way to Janaka's chamber, but hesitated when he arrived at the extravagant door embossed with leaves, flowers and birds of the forest. Even at this moment, in the depths of his anger, he was afraid of his brother. He clutched the tail of his long shawl in his right hand and stood still—the tinkling of his ornaments fell momentarily silent. He thought for some time, biting the tips of his fingernails. Then bracing himself, he pushed the heavy door open. Inside, he saw Janaka, pacing to and fro like a tiger, his shoulders hunched in anxious thought.

The creak of the hinges of the massive wooden door, brought the king to a halt. Janaka stopped in front of the opulent tapestries that adorned the walls of his chambers. They depicted memorable moments from the past four hundred years of his family's reign. He looked up and saw Kushadwaja, as if for the first time.

At last, he notices me, thought Kushadwaja, joining his palms and bowing slightly as a gesture of respect. 'Pranam, Brother!'

Squinting at Kushadwaja, Janaka nodded but said nothing. He could not understand how his little brother, so much younger than him, could have grown to be so handsome. In his early forties, Kushadwaja had the king's almond-shaped eyes, aquiline nose and fine black hair, but he stood straighter, was more regal in his bearing, and stronger. *Much like a king*, Janaka thought wistfully. Janaka had wasted many years attempting to mould him into a proper right hand. All that had proved useless. Kushadwaja remained indifferent to the palace's royal affairs. So Janaka had arranged Kushadwaja's marriage. The bride was Chandrabhaga, who was charmingly wise and outspoken. Soon after their union, she and Kushadwaja had two beautiful daughters. With Janaka's three children, they shared the indolence and golden glow of their childhood years.

It was Kushadwaja who spoke first. 'Oh, brother! We have only two weeks left now!' He knew he did not need to tell his brother the source of his worry. There was only a short time left to prepare for Princess Sita's swayamvar, where a long line of boldfaced suitors would contend to win her hand in marriage. It was not the first swayamvar they had held for Sita. The test that had been set for her suitors was a difficult one, and therefore, none had won her hand so far.

It was a major responsibility and it had been given to Kushadwaja only after a long test of time. Ever since the incident in the war against Kewatta three years ago, where Mithila lost two hundred men, King Janaka had not entrusted Kushadwaja with significant tasks.

Kushadwaja's heart pulsed in his ears. Only after much deliberation had he summoned the courage and strength to confront his brother. He had spent the last three weeks trying to plan the swayamvar for Sita, his niece and the king's eldest child. During the swayamvar, the princess' suitors would engage in a gruelling test to win her hand. Maintaining as princely a demeanour as possible, he suppressed thoughts of the sordid details of his past failure, steeled himself, and continued.

'You asked me to keep you informed.' He tried to maintain a soft and modulated tone, but the words spilled out in a choked voice. Janaka's gaze was on him, but Kushadwaja realized that his thoughts were elsewhere. His brother's face had become that of an old man, a stranger, with silver in his black hair, a drooping jawline, and an unruly and overgrown beard. The love in his eyes was absent, and the flesh that sagged from beneath his brows seemed to hang over them, making them smaller and duller.

So the rumours were true. Kushadwaja had heard that his brother had been acting strangely—always absorbed in thought and lost within the labyrinth of some immaterial question. It was unbecoming of a king to be of such a disposition.

Taking a deep breath, Kushadwaja fell into step with his pacing brother so that he was shoulder to shoulder with him—the younger prince's shoulder a bit higher and prouder than that of the king's. Janaka stopped, and turned his head slowly so that he could look his brother in the eye. His face was expressionless. Awareness flickered in his gaze as he took measure of Kushadwaja, who quelled the shudder that threatened him. The glint in his brother's expression was one he knew well. Sometimes, it happened that the king inexplicably knew things in advance.

Opening his mouth before his brother could, Kushadwaja spoke, 'You are the king of Mithila, brother, and the custodian of the Divine Bow. Your beloved daughter Sita has been unmarried too long, and I will see her engaged if you will let me. But you have not dispelled any of my concerns.' As he finished speaking, Kushadwaja uncomfortably glanced up at Janaka, who stood calmly beside him.

Unsettled, Kushadwaja swallowed thickly, wondering whether he had said too much. Janaka stood unmoved, as if the words floated towards him from across some great distance. His gaze, however, didn't waver from Kushadwaja's, although he arched his brows quizzically. An air of dissonance filled the space between them.

Blinking slowly, Janaka finally interrupted the silence, as if forcing words through his lips painfully. 'I remember. But you said you could be trusted to take care of everything.'

The word *trust* sank its sharp claws into Kushadwaja's heart. Overwhelmed by the pangs of guilt that the word provoked, his hold on his temper began to slip.

'But I can authorize nothing without your order, which I requested last week. You are yet to give me an answer. We have not arranged the guest quarters. The chief cook awaits your orders and funds for the materials. And what about the entertainers?'

Janaka began to pace again, following the same route from the upper level of his private chamber down to the lower chamber and to the window that overlooked the terrace. The eastern sun was breaking across the distant Himalayas and on his kingdom. He stopped at the turquoise ledge over the brilliant yellow terrace, satisfied with the sight of the sun breaking out over Mithila's verdant plains. Then, he turned and paced again. 'Do not worry. Things will be taken care of.'

Kushadwaja heaved a frustrated sigh, clenching his fists by his sides.

Janaka turned away dismissively, his expression distant and

devoid of emotion. It had been the same when he had been a young king, and Kushadwaja, just a boy. But his younger brother would not stand for it anymore. He strode across the room until he stood before his brother, unable to tolerate Janaka's loftiness for one more moment.

'Dear brother! What has happened to you?' His voice rose. 'We cannot seem to reach you. What has upset you?'

Janaka did not respond.

Kushadwaja grew quiet, staring at the man before him, at the person who now seemed like an empty shell. *Where is my brother? Is this the same man who taught me the value of responsibility?*

Finally, Kushadwaja said softly, 'I have told you this many times, brother. All I need is a word from you. If you allow me, I will take up the responsibilities and fulfil my duties.' The king's mind was so muddled with thoughts that he could not entertain his brother's pleas. It was true that the swayamvar was of absolute importance for the kingdom and his daughter. But he felt a sense of dread carving its way so deeply into his mind that he could not worry about anything else but the dream. 'Not now, my brother,' Janaka told Kushadwaja, his manner uncertain, placing a hand on his shoulder and glancing sympathetically at him. 'I will tell you when the time comes.'

Desperation seized Kushadwaja. His dignity had been torn from him. His hands ached from clenching his fists. He forced open his palms, but he could not erase the hurt from his voice. 'How long have I been asking for responsibility? You put me in charge of the swayamvar for Sita, and yet, you *dismiss* me without giving me the authority to execute that order.' His voice rose further, trembling, 'I have always wanted your support, but I can see now that it will never happen.'

Janaka stared into nothingness, slowly turning his vacant but subtly focused stare on his brother. 'Silence, Kushadwaja! You do not understand what is going on.'

'You think I am too ambitious, that I am hasty and make errors. You always remember what happened during the war with Kewatta. But, I am not that same person anymore.'

'What are you talking about?'

Kushadwaja lifted his chin. 'I know when I am made a fool of. Not only me, but I think everybody who has taken the swayamvar seriously is being made a fool of. Truth be told, you do not want Sita to marry.'

'That is untrue.' Janaka's voice was sharp. 'Kushadwaja, I'll not hear of any more such nonsense. I think your mind has been poisoned.' Janaka threw up his hands and looked at his brother.

'You have always said this. You feel that I am not worthy of my position. You think that I am easily swayed by others. I am deeply hurt that you do not have the confidence in me to fulfil my duties. It is *you* who is ignoring his responsibility by withdrawing into yourself.' Kushadwaja shifted his weight, as if to leave, and sighed, 'I will be of service when you require it.'

He turned to exit, pausing at the door, glancing back only to see his brother's distant gaze. 'Yesterday, an old woman with wild eyes, dishevelled hair, and in tattered clothes, came to the palace gates and demanded to meet the king. She claimed she had a great secret to pass on to you, but the guards did not allow her to enter. They tried to dismiss her, but she said she would not leave without telling the king what she knew.'

Kushadwaja continued, 'So they detained her and sent a message to me. I rushed to the gate and spoke to her.'

Motionless as stone, Janaka gazed at Kushadwaja, waiting to hear his next words.

'She was not ready to reveal the secret to me, but eventually I convinced her to tell me. She came, she said, to warn us that Ravana, the invincible Asura king of Lanka, would soon arrive in Mithila in disguise, and wreak havoc by abducting Sita.'

Pain sliced through Janaka's chest at these words. He struggled to catch his breath. He searched Kushadwaja's face, his brows knitting together anxiously.

'Why was she not sent to me?'

'She was just a mad old woman. Why do we need to take her seriously? I mentioned it to you only because it was about Sita.'

'What did she look like?'

'An old hag. They all look alike, don't they? Oh, now that I recall... She had only one eye.'

'And did she say anything else? Anything you remember?' Janaka asked with a slight tremble in his voice.

'Nothing of any import. The babblings of an old witch, shrieking on about warnings or something...'

Complete silence reigned for several moments. The despair-struck king stood bereft, as if that silence were ruling the kingdom. But Kushadwaja did not note the king's silence. Instead, he rubbed the spot between his eyes. Anger and humiliation throbbed within his head, and he briskly turned once more from the chamber, leaving his brother alone. The king did not notice and jumped at the echoing thud of the chamber door closing, a distant sound against the roar of his fears.

❋

For some time after his brother left, Janaka paced. Finally, when he grew tired, he sat down, trying to find some peace before finally giving up and walking towards the edge of his balcony, which overlooked his vast kingdom.

He surveyed it quietly. Mithila was bound on the north by the Himalayas, on the south by the river Ganges, on the east by the Kosala River, and on the west by the river Gandak. In the far distance, he could glimpse the Kosala and Gandak rivers as they snaked through the land, trailing away northward to the horizon, where the Himalayas rose to the heavens, cloaked in clouds still tinted pink with dawn.

From his window he saw the lovely orchard behind his palace, bearing rare and colourful fruits, filling the air with sweet, ripe scents: plantains, rose apples, jujube and mangoes. Trees bent low with plump fruits that had the complexion and softness of a girl's cheeks. He had always loved and cherished nature, and had never enjoyed hunting like other kings did. Trekking through the dense forest gave him the thrill of adventure. To him, every moment was one of survival amongst the unforeseen dangers lurking all around him.

Although Mithila did not have any rivers or other natural resources, Janaka more than made up for this lack, using his wisdom and ingenuity. Under his rule, the kingdom's water was stored in reservoirs and a thriving trade with other kingdoms added to its wealth. Often, jealous neighbours tried to wage war against Mithila, but Janaka and his trusted advisers' timely interventions thwarted all conflicts before they could threaten his kingdom. His resourcefulness and training in the art of war had secured victories against larger armies, such as in the battles against Kewatta and Chulani. The citizens of Mithila thrived in this prosperous and secure society. They held their king in highest esteem.

As the king return to pacing in his chamber, the tail end of his long shawl followed like an obedient pet. The attendants watched with a mixture of dismay and curiosity, awaiting his instructions. Janaka felt their eyes on his back.

'Leave me.'

They all but leapt for the door. The king was now left to his musings, alone.

Who is that old woman, and is there any truth to what she said? King Janaka wondered. He had been warned about Ravana, many times before. The demons, with their might and power, had been causing troubles for the kingdom for decades. Ravana could not risk an outright attack, but he could come in disguise and try to create chaos by abducting Sita. Janaka slowly wiped his sweaty palms on his shawl.

But is my brother right? Is the dream interfering with my duties? Kushadwaja's judgement is not dependable. He is spoilt and volatile and so much younger than me, that I sometimes forget he is my brother and not a little boy.

The Videha blood ran too thinly in his brother's veins. After their father had disappeared to the forest, Janaka had played the role of father and guru. Their mother had spoilt Kushadwaja, and when she died, she had left Janaka with a man who now slammed doors, after yelling at him, like a drunkard.

Janaka had been raised to be the ruler of Mithila from the day he was born. It had been passed down to him from prior generations, all the way back to Nimi, the first king of his tribe who had ruled the region along the Sarasvati river. They were the rulers of the Videha Dynasty, the Disembodied Beings, because their lineage upheld the importance of philosophy and detachment from worldly affairs despite ruling large kingdoms. Janaka had devoted himself to becoming a true Videha, practising hardships beyond the limits of his body, conquering temptations of the mind and the desires of the senses. He believed in a world beyond the ephemeral body, beyond earthly luxuries. Janaka was a seeker. His own journey towards self-realization was paramount in his mind, but he never disregarded his kingly duties, and he was a beloved king to his subjects. He often travelled through his kingdom, learning about his peoples' lives in the villages, their joys and troubles, often partaking in their rituals, ceremonies, weddings and funerals.

Now, Kushadwaja's outburst had made him reconsider the question. *Is life meant to be this endless fight over trivial matters?* He drifted back to his dream, holding on to the details because he knew in his heart, in some cryptic way, that the dream was a portent from the gods and that he must heed it. For a moment, standing in the middle of his opulent chamber, he felt as if he were a beggar again; with mud caking his hands and flies nesting in his hair, the riches of his kingdom suddenly emptied like water from a jar.

'A beggar or a king? Who am I?' he mumbled, as he began to pace again.

The wind blew in his ears and cold seeped into his bones. His years were growing short and the grizzled beard on his face, long. As he descended the stairs he felt his legs weaken, forcing him to sit down on a chair, breathing heavily.

Seated, he looked at everything that surrounded him—the hard white marble, the royal yellow curtains, the long corridor, the bright yellow balcony, the pink roses. Everything looked as if it were the reflection of a shallow pool. Nothing looked real. Everything seemed meaningless. Void of real existence, like bubbles in a stream. Everyone lied—the courtiers, the ministers, the guards, the chambermaids. Everyone... They were all performers in a meaningless show meant just to please him; but they were hollow inside, devoid of sincerity or genuineness.

He was deeply gripped by the fear of loneliness. He took a deep breath and closed his eyes. His posture straightened, his muscles stiffened, and in his mind he had a vision. Then, his eyes shot open and widened with a dazzling insight: his father had left this land like a beggar, with nothing in hand.

I carry the title of king, but all of this is ephemeral. Maybe life is like this. It is too short and fleeting, like a dream. But we are caught in the follies of the temporal world and do not see things as they truly are.

Janaka yearned for guidance. *How will I find my path?* He felt like a helpless infant, pushed out of a deep slumber with a jolt. *Am I now awakened? Who will hold the light to my steps?*

He walked to the balcony and leaned on the turquoise ledge, inhaling the fragrance of trailing pink roses that hung from saffron-coloured pots. The palace had been built high on a series of green terraces that descended to the great expanse of plains. From this vantage point, Janaka could see the palace orchards, the sunlit plains, the rolling foothills, the tangled forests of pungent camphor into which his father, grandfather and all of his ancestors back to the first king of his tribe, had disappeared.

In the camphor forest the trees grew thick, holding in shadows thick as blood. No one ventured near it except for the king himself. Most of his subjects felt its dark presence. Yet, for Janaka, it was a place of peace.

Beyond the trees, hidden from his sight, were the thoughts and the unspeakable desires of those who wished him ill. But, he could not hear their words as they whispered and plotted. If he could, he would be frozen with fear and disgust. Of all the words that were being uttered out there in the dark forests and wild borderlands, one word could be heard more than any other.

Not so much a word, as a name.

'Sita… Sita… Sita…'

Predictions

The roaring of a terrified crowd rose into a flood of commotion inside the palace. Thundering bangs on his door were followed by a roiling tide of intruders barging into his chamber. One of the men raised his sword at Janaka's neck. The king desperately tried to shield himself with his hands.

As the sword sliced through the air towards him, Janaka woke up. He sprang from his bed. Drenched in sweat, the cold marble under his feet jerked him back to his senses. Had it been a dream? Or was it real? He wasn't sure anymore.

Swallowing against the dry, thickness of his throat, he picked up the clay pot from the side table and drank. The cold water brought Janaka more sharply into the waking world. Slowly, he walked towards the balcony. Placing his elbows on the balcony rail and resting his head on his palms, he gazed out at the dark line on the horizon. The cold northern breeze touched his face, and a tingling chill passed through his body. His heart was gripped with an ominous fear. He was at a loss. He felt as if he were coming apart. What was happening to him?

✵

'It is a sign of impending calamity!'

Sage Satananda's gnarled arthritic hands were permanently curled into semi-circles like crescent moons. In Janaka's great hall, wearing only a loincloth, he sat on his haunches in the place of honour beside the king. His thin chest, turned reddish-brown by the sun, looked as if it had been dusted with white powder. His bald head shone like a dark garnet. The other three sages, Pukkusa, Seneka and Devinda sat at the foot of the raised dais. No one had taken the king's dream lightly.

It was midday now. The bright sun shone through long windows on the wall, which admitted sunshine and fresh air. These windows were carved in the shapes of animals and plants, causing strange but beautiful shadows to fall on the turquoise- and gold-enamelled tiles. The shadows of a flower and that of a rearing lion moved across the floor in an unearthly dance of their own.

The sages were the four pillars of Janaka's kingdom. They kept him centred and strong on the foundation that his ancestors had built.

'Are you certain of this?' asked Janaka, insistent. Immediately, Pukkusa, a short, plump man who looked far younger than his years, began talking of another dream he had recently heard of, from one of the villagers who had come to him for advice. The villager had also dreamt of disaster and attack by neighbouring kingdoms. Everyone, including Satananda, nodded wisely.

Devinda, the youngest and most inexperienced sage, leaned forward and asked about the king's diet: had he eaten almonds close to bedtime? Almonds can cause strange dreams, he foolishly ventured. At that, Satananda's lips pursed with disapproval. Devinda sat up straight again, sheepishly trying to regain his dignity.

'Are there any other signs? We must keep a sharp eye out for them,' Janaka stated, in an uneven voice.

'It can be many things—drought, war, or any other chaos.' Beneath their drooping, wrinkled lids, Satananda's eyes shone.

His voice was steady and earnest.

Pukkusa leaned forward again and exclaimed, 'Oh, my lord! Do not underestimate your dream. It is no doubt a strong portent of some disaster. There have been many other omens of concern—shakunas, phenomena that inform us of change. Besides the old woman who spoke to Kushadwaja, there is news of a two-headed calf being recently born in a village.'

Devinda, joining the chorus of admonitions, was happy to affirm these reports of bad omens. 'My lord, last week, one of the villagers from Mayavila saw some animals running away from the forest. And in Pukkusa's own home, a grove of young fruit trees had been twisted with the black rot.'

'Just this morning as I walked to the court, I found a dead crow in my path,' Seneka, the tall, quiet one, added. 'These are all unusual events. It would be unwise to simply dismiss them.'

Satananda nodded gravely. 'My lord, you know what the Vedic texts say—that the planets in the universe radiate energy. There is definitely a correlation between what is happening above and what is happening on earth. The soul of the universe has its own ways and means to communicate. You must not ignore what the universe tells you!' Again, the three other sages nodded in unison.

They are always like that, the king thought sullenly. The sages never disagreed with one another. It was as if they worked as one mind. None brought forth a new idea by themselves. Once they arrived at a general consensus, there could be no disagreement and each would defend the consensus as if it were his own idea.

'Is the dream a premonition of what is going to happen?' Janaka, desperate to quell his disquietude, studied the faces of the sages.

'Yes, you could say that,' Satananda said. 'We arrive at these interpretations based on our years of experience, knowledge and understanding of the signs. Don't you remember that we have had many such in the past?' Satananda asked in a patronizing tone, as if speaking to a child.

'I must confirm what we assume in this. It is crucial. How can we ascertain it?' The king could not hide the desperation in his voice.

Seneka sighed. His voice shifted to an intimate whisper, the voice he used when speaking of hidden truths, a way of speaking that sounded like the sweet birdsong in the king's private courtyard. 'The Vedas say that dreams can never be disassociated from our lives. They are an integral part of who we are; another facet which is unseen, just like the other side of a coin. During the course of our dreams, our soul releases our unlived and suppressed life. In order to avoid chaos, what we don't express in our lives, later appears in our dreams,' he said, with a sense of pride in his authority and eloquence.

'The gods are communicating to you through dreams,' Devinda interjected.

Infuriated, the king smashed his hand against the arm of the throne. In an ill-tempered voice, he said, 'I understand that! But how do we know that this is a real forewarning? What are the other ways to understand it?'

Seneka met the king's gaze. 'The only way to understand and be certain of what the universe is trying to show us is through divination. We need to perform a yagna. That will give us more certainty.' Seneka was a proud man, and he could barely conceal the indignation in his voice. He thought he was much wiser than Janaka, but not as wise as Satananda, of course.

'I have had too much of people's pride lately,' Janaka muttered, thinking of his brother. He got up from his throne and walked towards the doorway. Although his heart was still ill at ease, he turned and walked back, to stand before the four sages. 'In this, you cannot be wrong.'

Satananda's eyes bulged for a moment. He was unused to the king questioning his authority, but when he spoke, his tone remained calm, 'Must we remind you of the poor fortune of the king of Vaishali? The priests warned him of the forthcoming drought he'd seen in a dream, but he ignored their guidance. Many weeks later, he believed it when animals dropped in their tracks in the burning jungles and amidst the parched grasslands. The poor died, the rich died, the rivers ran dry, and the sun burned brighter than it had in a thousand years. I plead with you, my lord; let us not ignore these warning signs.'

Janaka was tormented, not by the fear of invading armies, but by the image of his kingdom gripped by drought. He placed his right hand on his forehead, rubbing his temples as if trying to stop an imminent headache.

Satananda continued, 'We need to hold a yagna.'

Janaka rubbed his wrist with restless fingers. He nodded his head a few times and felt signs of disapproval creeping onto his face. The ceremonies would be as always, expensive and time-consuming.

'Fine,' he muttered. 'We will see what we can do.'

The sages' hearts aligned in discomfort at the insincerity in the king's voice.

Janaka began pacing the hall. The sages looked on, impassive. The king felt meaning could be derived from all signs and most dreams. But the inexplicable dread of a disaster approaching eclipsed all these signs and dreams. Almost like a forewarning. *It is possible that our mind is a miniature of the universe. It behaves the way the universe behaves. When the world outside is in chaos, the same thing happens in the mind. All of these things together could not lie. Could they?* He raised his eyebrows, looked at Seneka and the others once again. The shadow of his scepticism darkened their faces. He pulled his shawl closer, though there was no wind.

'We shall also ask somebody else,' Janaka announced.

Satananda stood stunned, his features expressing his shock, his mouth silent, speechless. It was Pukkusa who countered. 'We can't delay it till we find a good dream interpreter, my lord! This dream is a strong portent. A yagna—'

'I said you will have your yagna,' the king snapped, 'but I must speak to Mahosadha.'

The four sages looked at each other with doubt and disbelief, their own scepticism clouding their faces. Mahosadha was a good man, loyal to the king, but he was not one of them. He was untutored in the Vedas. He had a good head for practical affairs, but not wisdom. Yet this was the way of their king, they knew. The king saw his duties as both spiritual and practical, and he would never find an adviser who could handle both realms. And so, the sages who understood their place, never complained openly about Mahosadha. Instead, they satisfied themselves by grumbling once they were out of the king's earshot.

Satananda recovered first. He said in his silky smooth voice, 'We are interpreting a most complex prediction. So it is around your wisdom that we orbit, just as the seas follow the waxing and waning of the moon; and just as weary travellers rest in the shades of trees, whose cooling boughs eclipse the sun's fervid rays and fan the sweltering air.'

The sage paused and resumed. 'But infused with such unbounded intelligence and power, does your Excellency truly need Mahosadha's counsel? Mahosadha, granted, is an invincible warrior and minister, an unexcelled army chief! But his judgements touch only temporal affairs! Who can find fault that his realm is merely in the physical plane, even if a person confined to that realm of awareness cannot look beyond it and open himself up to possibilities of—'

'Correct!' Janaka interrupted; his face hardening. 'Mahosadha deals with empirical facts and logic.' He was aware that the only way to untangle the true secret of the universe was through the yagna ceremony. But he trusted Mahosadha's acumen too. He knew that the gods may speak through signs, but who are those pure souls who can interpret them? Were Satananda and the other sages really pure if they felt threatened by someone as pragmatic as Mahosadha? It was because of their insecurity that they had objected to Mahosadha being his adviser in the first place.

The king doubted if he could find the guidance he sought, in the palace. He would have to trust in himself until he found what he needed.

'This discussion is over for now,' he told the sages. He sat down heavily on the floor, staring at nothing as if he were alone, as if the sages were indeed no more than four lifeless planets constellating around a void.

Hesitantly, Pukkusa spoke, 'My lord! Besides these portents, there are more unfortunate happenings across our kingdom. I am sure you are aware of this!'

Janaka glanced enquiringly at Pukkusa.

'Tataka and Subahu in the Bhayanak Van, have killed more sages this week,' Pukkusa said with a grimace.

Tataka and Subahu were demons, a mother and son, who had been ambushing and terrorizing travellers who dared to pass through the Bhayanak Van, the Forest of Fear, near the river Ganges, opposite the Sarayu river. Long ago, they had been cursed by Sage Agastya and had been transformed into demons with cannibalistic natures and terrifying forms. Since then, they had vowed their revenge on all sages, and as a source of food, had turned to hapless travellers.

Tataka's foul presence made even the Ganges river unclean. Her very existence, and that of her son, had been nothing but a source of fear for the people of Mithila.

Many sages, including the effulgent Vishwamitra, considered by many to be the most powerful sage of all time, had many times been subject to the demons' harassment. Whenever the great sages go to the forest to perform their rituals, Tataka had tormented them. She possessed the strength of a thousand elephants. She was fearless and felt no qualms about attacking even unarmed sages. She was free to wreak havoc because she had the support of the all-powerful Ravana. The neighbouring kings did not dare attack her, fearful of her ferocity.

It dawned on Janaka that he had many challenges to meet. He felt exhausted and battered. His philosophical quest had tired his mind. His spiritual craving had weakened his soul.

The Wise Minister

'The dream, my lord, is only a fantasy. It has nothing to do with reality. I believe dreams are fleeting and mean nothing. That's why they never stay with us for long. They appear in our minds when we are in deep sleep. We should not take them seriously unless the illusion is helpful,' Mahosadha declared.

Behind the heavy doors of the prime minister's office, Mahosadha and his king were taking an afternoon snack of sweetmeats and glasses of *mantha*—dry barley meal stirred into milk. Young serving girls fanned them. Mahosadha finished his last sweetmeat, set down his plate, and added, 'Maybe it is time to strengthen the army.'

Mahosadha was much younger than the four sages. His birth had been predicted by learned men, including the sages themselves. He had been born the son of Sumana, the wife of a prosperous merchant. Mahosadha displayed great wisdom as a child and had matured at an unimaginable speed. A prodigy, he possessed architectural talents that astounded the best engineers in the city at the age of seven. Before his twentieth birthday, he had built an architectural marvel looking over lakes filled with lotuses: a hall of extraordinary beauty with interesting nooks and crannies that held myriad birds and flowers. Mahosadha had made a gift of the great hall to the king. It was Janaka's introduction to the young man. Once he saw the beauty and ingenuity of the hall, he had asked the sages to bring Mahosadha before him so that they could speak in person.

It was when they heard of Mahosadha's meeting with the king, that the royal sages realized he might someday become a threat to their power. The sages had been insecure and jealous of him since then, and had done everything in their power to halt his rising influence. All four had said to the king, as if in unison, 'O Lord! Do not think to make him your minister. Not unless we first test his ability with complex problems and monitor his character closely.'

But instead of testing him, Janaka had asked Mahosadha's advice on concerns about Mithila's defence. Mahosadha's guidance had proved as elegant and shrewd as his architectural productions. The king had been pleased. As prime minister, Mahosadha proved a great statesman, a cunning war strategist, and most importantly, the best man for the position. For what better man deserved the highest diplomatic position in the land than one who could outwit, outmanoeuvre and outclass four angry, conniving royal sages—and for twenty years? In doing so, Mahosadha had often steered the king away from their selfish schemes. Mahosadha even seemed to enjoy the challenge, and so Janaka had come to rely on his relentless pragmatism and logic.

Now, in the minister's chambers, Janaka felt refreshed after the repast and by listening to his minister's words. He took comfort in listening to Mahosadha, who always seemed to have an answer for everything under the sun. As far as Mahosadha was concerned, everything had a cause and reason, and the cause was always earthly, not heavenly. For every problem, there was, without doubt, a solution, and it was something one could see and sense.

Yet today, though he felt comforted, Janaka was still uneasy.

He could not help but remember what the sages had said. Could there really be an answer to all the questions in the world?

Mahosadha stood, awaiting an answer. As usual, the prime minister wore an earth-coloured upper cloth, cinched at the waist with a sash. He wore a simple coronet of gold on his head. His posture reflected the firmness of his opinion, his every action or inaction seemed deliberate, and the expression on his hard, masculine face was unmarred by doubt. The king felt none of the familiar discomfort that affected him when he was with the sages, for he knew that even if he did not take Mahosadha's advice, the man would not care. He would not sulk for days. Instead, he would accept the decision and set his mind to the next task. For that reason, there was a perfect balance between them.

'Don't you think that these dreams could intimate some sort of communication from the infinite? Is there even one event in the world that might occur without a reason?' The king asked.

'That may be, but I believe that what is more important is what appears in front of us. Why should we act upon dreams when we have so much more to challenge and master in this world?' Mahosadha asked, in his naturally confident tone.

'What you do not understand is that this was no ordinary dream. What followed after the dream was coherent and exactly as what I experienced in it—even the same threats and the same words. That old woman at the gates...what if it is a portent of misfortune? I cannot help being apprehensive.' Janaka's voice reflected the worry that continued to grow in his heart.

'I understand your spiritual thirst and search. I am sure there are many saints and sages who can guide you to discover the answers you seek. But I am not sure that the sages of the court can help you in your journey. I think they try to create a frenzy about the supernatural, rather than focussing on the pursuit of wisdom. All they are is a drain on the treasury. Every time they need answers, they suggest an expensive yagna. Yagnas are time-consuming and extravagant, and require rivers of ghee. Ask them if it will rain this afternoon, and they will say "O Lord, let us hold a yagna for that!" It happens every time!' Mahosadha finished bitterly.

Janaka was surprised that he did not spit on the ground. But that was Mahosadha. He did not mince words. Today was no different. Usually he praised Mahosadha for this, because he felt that only people who were sincere could speak boldly. But today, the king turned away to hide his scowl. After all, his minister too, was not without prejudice. Mahosadha must have thought he, the king, would rather take the sages' advice, Janaka thought to himself. That his logic was being undermined by his dreams and what the sages proclaimed.

I must trust myself, Janaka thought for the second time that day. He turned back to his prime minister.

'Mahosadha, you must believe that I value your opinion. However, as a king, I have to balance both ends of the scale. The people of Mithila trust the sages. If they make a proclamation, it is almost impossible for me to deny it. Even though I value their opinions less than I do yours, I believe that the dream is an important manifestation from the divine. It would be irrational of me to not explore it further.'

He struggled to find the right words. 'Everything that happens is for a reason, and everything is connected to everything else,' Janaka added, feeling as if he were seeking approval from Mahosadha.

He continued. 'All such signs are indicators of forecasted

events, and they are connected to the soul of the universe. The stars, omens and signs, come from the universe. We can choose to accept them as they are. Or we can choose to take the reins in our hands, interpret these portents, go deeper within ourselves, become one with the universe, and influence the origin. Either way, whatever you believe, it will come true for you,' said Janaka.

'How would you achieve this, Maharaj?' asked Mahosadha curiously.

'That is what I do not truly know. How can I find the path? Can I discover it myself? Maybe I need the right guru to guide me.'

'Whatever you feel is right, Maharaj,' Mahosadha spoke calmly, as if to brush the conflict aside. Janaka got the impression that Mahosadha may have felt slighted and had spoken only to reassure him. 'Mahosadha, my valued companion, I have always respected your opinion and advice. I cannot think of anyone else as prime minister of Mithila. You have shown diplomatic acumen as a statesman, and when all diplomatic means have been exhausted, you are a good strategist in many wars.' Mahosadha seemed appeased. He tilted his head and looked at the king directly in the eyes. 'Thank you so much for your recognition, my Lord. But it is unnecessary. I understand that you have given me much importance and it has attracted much envy. You need to show impartiality towards your advisers, so by all means, I advise you to go forward with the yagna.'

'Yes. I also think so. Absolutely,' Janaka said firmly. He waited a moment longer after speaking, holding his minister's gaze, searching for some hint of deceit or disloyalty.

As always, he found none. Yet, he couldn't shake off his feeling of disquiet. The minister's tone had been smooth, making his words almost ring hollow. This only served to trouble Janaka even more.

✽

Near the fireplace made of clay stones set out on the palace terrace, Janaka sat in the lotus position. The four court sages—Satananda, Seneka, Pukkusa and Devinda—sat around the fire. Pukkusa, the *adhvarya*—assistant to the main priest—had measured the ground and built the stone altar. Seneka was the *hotar* this time—the leader of the yagna. Satananda had refused to lead the yagna in silent protest against the king's meeting with Mahosadha. It was petty and foolish of him, and with a petulant expression on his face he sat down for the holy ritual.

It was a beautiful, cool evening, calm and free. The holy time was as tranquil as a yogi breathlessly anchored in infinity. In the distance, melodies from a bamboo flute sweetened the air with an evening hymn. As the hours crept on, the moon rose. Seneka, as *hotar*, sat closest to the fire, so close that he could feel its radiance. The king and his sages sat in a half-moon pattern, and behind them, dozens of people had gathered. Before them were baskets of rare green herbs and mounds of flowers in red, blue and yellow. In Vedic Sanskrit, Seneka began chanting the mantras of the *Samaveda*. The others repeated after him, their voices rising and falling, rising and falling again, resonant and rhythmic, and their nostrils flaring with the effort to maintain a steady breathing that rose from deep in the belly. All the while they poured ghee and offered herbs to the flames.

The fire swallowed the offerings with its divine mouth which opened to the infinite, radiating an energy that the king felt vibrating in his bones. At times, white smoke shot up with a hiss, drifting upward towards the thousand stars of the night.

Everything thrown into the fire was reaching the heavens. The people in the gathering were overcome, and they trembled; the divine power touched them. In turn, more ghee, milk, sesame, grains, cakes and *soma*—the divine wine, were offered to the leaping flames. Satananda kept his eyes closed as the divine spirit filled him, opening them only to throw handfuls of various powders on to the stones, feeding the blaze until the fire stood up like a giant.

The white smoke was so thick the king could not see his own hands before him. He was now enchanted and felt warm and comfortable. He closed his eyes, yet in his mind's eye, he could see the others nearby.

Satananda, his eyes still closed, left his place by the fire. He stood up, arms outstretched, swaying back and forth under the moon. Turning abruptly towards Janaka, he crouched beside him and whispered in his ear. Janaka began to shiver as a chill crept into his bones. The news was simple:

'A great terror is about to befall your kingdom.'

Sita

Janaka entered the great hall, where preparations were taking place for the swayamvar. Queen Sunayana, Janaka's wife, her beauty undiminished by the years, was busy overseeing everything. Janaka's daughter Urmila was also there, as were Kushadwaja's daughters. All rose from their seats as a gesture of respect when Janaka entered.

'Where is Sita? I have not seen her since this morning,' Janaka asked.

'Did she not come to you? I thought she was with you,' replied Sunayana raising her head, a hint of concern in her voice. 'I saw her during the morning prayers. She said she was going to have her dress fitted and then surprise you.'

She beckoned one of the chambermaids and questioned her about Sita's whereabouts. The girl shook her head and nervously told the queen that she had not seen her, either.

'She must have gone somewhere. Now that I thought about it, it seemed as if something was bothering her,' said Sunayana.

'What could be on her mind, Sunayana?' Janaka asked worriedly, remembering what the old woman outside the gates had told Kushadwaja about Ravana.

'Everyone in the palace is eagerly awaiting the upcoming celebration. But if there is one person who is not, it is her,' replied Sunayana.

'I don't understand, Sunayana,' said Janaka, with an

increasingly apprehensive expression on his face.

Sunayana was a quiet voice of reason. 'I don't think we need to be worried. I have seen Sita unhappy many times and her response is always the same. She wants to be alone, to sit in a quiet place and brood. But she would not go far. She must be somewhere in the palace.'

Urmila, Janaka's younger daughter, who resembles her mother both in looks and in her calm, reasonable attitude, spoke, 'Oh, Father! If Sita is unhappy I believe I know why.'

Janaka, Sunayana, and the other girls turned to listen intently.

'Of late, I have noticed that she has been always gloomy when the subject of the swayamvar comes up. I don't think she is happy with the idea of marrying just anyone who wins the bow test,' said Urmila.

Sunayana interrupted. 'This swayamvar is Sita's fate. It is not a choice. She was truly a gift. She has all the blessings in the world—yet she is not happy and perhaps never will be. Destiny has favoured our kingdom from the moment she has been with us, but it has never been favourable to her.'

Mandavi, Kushadwaja's youngest and shyest daughter, then piped up.

'I think it is something else altogether.'

Sunayana turned towards her.

'What is it about, then?' she asked, curious.

'I think she has her heart set on someone.'

'Who?' Sunayana's voice grew shrill.

'Rama, the prince of Ayodhya.'

Sunayana's eyes widened. 'Prince Rama? But how do they know each other? Where have they met?'

'Do you remember the time we all went to Sage Vasishta's

gurukul for our studies? Rama and Sita met there at the gurukul and they spent time together.'

Srutakirti interrupted. 'I don't think so. Sita and I are very close and she usually discusses everything with me. I can honestly say she has never talked about Rama. If he is anywhere in her heart, she would have told me about it.'

Suddenly Janaka froze, as if lightning had struck him.

'It has just dawned upon me,' he said. 'I know where she is. I will go and find her.'

Janaka knew that she would be in the Kshatriya Gopura, the topmost tower of the palace and the highest point in Mithila. The sudden realization gave him some relief. But he still felt a sense of dread. However, he knew there was no point in worrying until he had climbed up the Kshatriya Gopura and seen for himself whether Sita was there or not.

Hurriedly, he started up the stairs to the palace tower, a glorious symbol of Arya architecture. The tower, which stood like a lance pointing upwards to the sky, was visible from a great distance, standing watch over Janaka's kingdom. At the top, it was shaped like a dome, but the space within was so small that it could barely fit three people. During times of war, guards would occupy the tower to watch the horizon for approaching enemies. The kingdom, however, was presently at peace and the tower was now an ideal place for Sita to be alone.

Halfway up the stairs, Janaka found himself out of breath. He had to stop for a while. Looking out of one of the many windows of the tower's stairwell, memories came flooding back to him. He remembered how Sita had come into their lives. It had all started with the drought.

❋

At that time, Janaka had been a childless king. It had been many seasons since it rained in his kingdom. With no rain, the crops failed. And with nothing to eat, many people and animals starved. Every day, people from the city would come to appeal to him and it tore him up that there was nothing he could do to save them. They fell like flies and it broke his heart. One day, in the midst of this famine and drought, the sages carried out a divine invocation that unveiled a prophecy—prosperity would return to the land only if he, the young king, ploughed the land himself.

Janaka, of course, agreed. So, witnessed by all of his sages and courtiers, he picked up a spade and started to work at the hard soil. But the earth was so dry that the spade recoiled, giving back a sound as if it was striking rock.

The chief sage then said, 'Maharaj. You have to try harder. Mother Earth will surely be pleased with you and the people of Mithila.'

Janaka doubled his efforts and kept hammering at the solid earth with his spade. Sweat started pouring from his body, glistening in the scorching sunlight. The soil was hot and hard and gave off fumes in the sunlight. He quickly became exhausted. When he straightened his spine and looked up at the sky, to see if he was to receive a reward for his efforts, the sun was still burning like a ball of fire, merciless and relentless. Then he lowered his eyes to the horizon. There, the sky was growing dark, with thick clouds rolling in. All of a sudden, a cold wind began to blow. Before anyone knew what was happening, thunder reverberated and lightning swung its sword across the sky, illuminating the earth and throwing darts of fear into the hearts of men. But this spectacle did not portend the end of the world as many of the onlookers thought it did; rather, it heralded the beginning of a new era, as sweet rain started showering down upon the barren land of Mithila.

The smell of the new rain mixed with that of the soil created an aroma of freshness, dampness and of life itself. It brought joy to the hearts of the people, and they began to dance.

The chief sage, Satananda, exclaimed, 'Maharaj! Mother Earth is pleased. This is the beginning of a new age of prosperity for Mithila.'

Still looking out of the window, Janaka remembered what happened next as if it were yesterday.

Overjoyed at the rain, he returned to the spade. But just as he was about to dig deep into the earth once more, he noticed something in the furrow he had just ploughed. Now filled with water, a largish object caught his eye. He bent to inspect it, and found a bamboo cradle wedged in the soil. To his astonishment, a baby girl lay inside, beaming up at him. The childless Janaka crouched and picked up the infant with both his hands, dazzled at the sight of her. As bright and as sudden as the lightning which had just flashed across the sky, Janaka realized what had happened—a maiden had appeared as the result of his invocation to the goddess of the earth. Yes, this could be the answer to a long and ardent prayer, a blessing to remove the long curse of drought and a portent of prosperity to come!

Satananda had then said to him, 'Maharaj! Raise this child as your own. She is a gift from the goddess of the earth and the harbinger of your kingdom's prosperity. She should be named Sita.'

Queen Sunayana took Sita in her arms, holding the baby close to her bosom, as she showered her with kisses. Tears of joy sprang from her eyes.

Satananda then pronounced, 'Wherever young Sita goes, that place will flourish.'

And all of Satananda's predictions of that time came true. Some said that Sita was the reincarnation of a goddess, a gift from a god, a harbinger of blessings. But irrespective of her divine antecedents, little Sita still cried with the innocence of an ordinary child. When her mother held her close, she became quiet.

People often asked: *Where does Sita come from? Who are her real parents? Is she an apsara descended from heaven? Is she a divine gift uncovered from the earth, sprung from the goddess of prosperity?*

Sita was an enigma, just like her birth. However, everyone agreed on one thing—upon Sita's arrival, Mithila started flourishing with wealth and prosperity, and her fame spread across the land.

As a child, she shone like a jewel and as she grew, she was the embodiment of beauty. Sunayana carried pride for her eldest daughter deep in her heart. Sita's sister, Urmila, and Kushadwaja's daughters Srutakirti and Mandavi—all loved her, constantly vying for her attention. Yet Sita was humble and gentle. There was something special about her. It emanated from within her, a radiant fire that came from her soul, a love and thirst for life.

Janaka woke from this warm memory and found himself still standing halfway up the stairs of the Kshatriya Gopura. After the first few levels, the stone staircase began to curl up sharply. He ran up the remaining flights of the stairway to see if his precious Sita was at the top of the tower.

Janaka's instincts were right. Sita was there, standing at the edge of the overlook, staring out at the land. Janaka gasped for air, winded after the climb. He waited, catching his breath, trying to figure out what to say to his beloved child. Sita turned and saw him.

'Oh, Father, what happened? Is something the matter?'

Janaka paused, calming down somewhat.

He then got to the heart of the matter. 'Sita, are you not happy? Are you truly dreading the thought of another swayamvar?'

'No, Father, it is not that. What I want is not important.

What is destined to happen should happen. What the sages predicted should happen.' Sita went silent, and Janaka did not ask anything more.

Janaka joined her at the overlook and gazed out. He had brought Sita up here many times when she was a child. Together, they had admired this magnificent kingdom from that same vantage point. From that height, so many things were visible: the city, the grand spectacle of Mithila and the horizon. Below them, people looked like dolls, perfect miniatures. They were going about their daily lives. That image of the city, the whole kingdom reduced to miniatures on a game board, could sometimes evoke life's biggest questions and dilemmas. Like the role of a king or the relationship between a king and his people. It was here that Janaka had begun to teach Sita some of the great lessons of philosophy, where they exchanged great ideas and lofty notions, her young mind always inquisitive and bright.

Janaka recalled a discussion he had once had with Sunayana.

'She is extraordinary,' Janaka had insisted. 'There is something special about her. It emanates from within her; she is without equal.'

'Yes, but someday she must marry,' Sunayana had answered. And that was the beginning of his second great fear: losing his Sita to marriage.

She was his daughter. But she was also a confidante and a symbol of the kingdom's prosperity. Without her, Janaka knew that his palace would feel large and empty. But he had no intention of refusing her happiness, merely for the sake of his own.

'I must let go of her someday, Sunayana. It is the order of things, as much as it pains me,' he said, adding, 'Such is the plight of a father and a king.'

Uddalaka's Revelation and Mahosadha's Predicament

'Oh, Father! Please stop him from going. I cannot lose him like I lost my husband.'

Sujata glanced at Uddalaka's worn face, his wrinkles folded in perplexity, and silently pleaded that her father could make Ashtavakra stay.

'I have already decided to go to the palace. I want to know what happened to my father. I cannot wait anymore...' The boy faltered, his voice catching as a shudder wracked his body, tight with barely repressed agitation. He strained to control the balance of his torso, struggling against his warring body to maintain a firm posture with his stick.

Uddalaka remained calm, his wrinkles smooth now and devoid of emotion as he looked at Sujata. His demeanour made no sense. She could not comprehend why her father was taking the matter lightly. Finally, after a few moments of quiet, a small smile crinkled Uddalaka's face, as if he had been preparing for this moment for a long time.

'It is fine, Sujata. Let him go. We cannot stop him anymore.'

'But, Father! He is only fourteen years old. And he is frail and—'

Uddalaka raised his hand to hush her. 'Do not worry. Nothing will happen to him. Your love for him has made you blind and you are unable to see the greatness in him. He is not an ordinary boy. He is an enlightened being. Nothing can stop him from going. There is tremendous strength within his frail body, and he will excel at everything with his power. He has a mission in his life, and you must let him go to fulfil it. He is destined for this. It will be unwise of you to stop him.'

'But you must stop him! He will be killed, just as his father was,' Sujata cried out, panic squeezing her chest.

'Who told you his father was killed? That is only your assumption. That's what all of us believed until today.'

'Are you saying that he could still be alive?' Her heart jumped with hope. Was it possible? Unable to control herself, she stuttered, 'Then, why has he not come back?'

'That is what your son has to find out,' Uddalaka said. 'I truly believe that King Janaka would not kill innocent people. The Videha kings have a tradition of respecting saints, as they themselves are saint-kings, Rajarshis. I have come to know recently, that he has been seeking advice from sages on how to bring ahimsa to his kingdom. The Vedas and the Upanishads speak of the value of ahimsa, of not hurting or killing anybody. All living beings are divine, and we all are connected to each other. Hurting another is hurting oneself.'

Ashtavakra and Sujata looked at Uddalaka curiously.

'King Janaka has a bigger mission in life, apart from his duties as the king of Mithila,' he continued. 'His twenty-four forefathers before him merely ruled the kingdom. But Janaka's path holds greater things for him.'

'What is that?' Ashtavakra asked.

'Over the decades, the Asuras have posed threats to Janaka and his kingdom because they have constantly competed for power with humans. Asuras are demigods with capabilities beyond that of humans. They possess great spiritual prowess as well. However, they are inclined to destroy every good creation with their devastating powers and have always provoked wars with kings on earth.

'Janaka vowed to protect his kingdom from their forces. But there is one demon, Ravana, the Asura king who surpasses Janaka's capabilities and who has taken an oath to destroy Mithila.'

Uddalaka continued, 'I have heard recently that the king had a strange dream and he believes it has a purpose. The sages and people all over the kingdom have tried interpreting it, but the king is unhappy with these interpretations. His close confidante and prime minister disregarded the dreams. But Janaka is still looking for the right person to help him.'

The old man stroked his long beard, and for the briefest second disappeared into his thoughts. He shifted on his mat and looked directly at his grandson.

'Ashtavakra, I believe you can do this. You can help him find the right answer. This may be the right time for you to go to him.'

Uddalaka turned to his grandson and saw that Ashtavakra was deep in contemplation, an awareness of what must be done written on his face.

'You need to enter the palace and tell them that you have come to reveal the secret of the dream that the king had. It is your duty, Ashtavakra, to get rid of the king's entanglements and rescue him from these worries. The kingdom of Mithila needs him.' He paused.

'Janaka has attracted too many enemies, being the custodian of both the magical bow and his daughter, Sita. The people of the neighbouring kingdoms believe this is the reason that Mithila is flourishing. He is surrounded by sages who are sycophants, and he needs the right advice to lead the kingdom out of this situation.'

Ashtavakra let out a huge sigh. He nodded his head in agreement. It held all the weight of the task he had been asked to perform.

❊

Meanwhile, back at the palace, Mahosadha was disturbed, but with very good reason. He feared for the very survival of the kingdom. Earlier that morning, he had met with Senapati Mahadev and the other brigadiers. Mahosadha could still hear Mahadev's words ringing in his ears.

'Respected Mahosadha!' Mahadev had said. 'We have received news from our spies that Sudhanvan, the king of Sankasya, is preparing for an attack. He may come here to disrupt the swayamvar, which offers us little time. We must increase our preparations twofold and fortify ourselves against any attack. However, the king has ordered the exact opposite. He has asked us to make further cuts to the army.'

Shocked by what he had heard, Mahosadha had rushed to the king's chamber seeking clarification. But his sense of urgency had not been reciprocated. He stood in the corridor outside the king's chamber, fingering the gold-plated coronet on his head and then taking it off, holding it in one hand while tracing its pattern with the fingers of the other, and then putting it back on again. When he was tired of standing, he would sit on the chair placed outside the chamber, cooling himself with a small handheld fan. Then, when he grew tired of sitting, he would pace. This was unbearable for a man of action like Mahosadha.

What is going on inside? Mahosadha wondered. *What could*

be more important than the safety of the kingdom? What is the king doing? He had better not be spending even more time with his sages...

Mahosadha began to pace even more restlessly. How could a respected Videha king be so without a sense of responsibility, with the threat of war looming over his kingdom? Mahosadha continued his brisk pacing, wringing his hands as his head began to ache with the ludicrousness of it all. Could Janaka have been influenced by the sages in the palace? He sat down again and stared at the wall. It was one thing for the king to spend time on spiritual pursuits, but to risk the kingdom itself!

Mithila had fought wars and survived, yes, but always after weeks, if not months of strategic planning and preparation. Mahosadha could see clearly what needed to be done, but there was nothing he could do without Janaka's command. At the very least, he must convince the king to acknowledge the impending threat.

But instead of sitting and planning his defensive strategy, the king has been spending his valuable time with sages! And now, he has actually ordered cuts to the army!

Mahosadha wrung his hands, deeply distressed by what was happening. He knew exactly what real life involved. He had seen too many men die in agony, run through by spears, trampled by elephants and hacked to death by swords. Yet it was the sacrifices made by those very same men that allowed the people of Mithila to bask in the freedom that they were enjoying now. Mahosadha was baffled that Janaka did not give this fact the importance it was due.

Mahosadha was not one to draw attention to himself. Some men prefer to work in the shadows and stay out of the limelight. He was one such man. Strategy was his strength and he was skilled at using it to turn adverse situations to his advantage.

During the war with Kampila, he had gathered intelligence about King Kewatta, forging alliances and using espionage to turn these new allies against each other. Then, anticipating the enemy would cut the water supply to the city, he had dug huge, deep wells and filled reservoirs, so that Mithila could withstand a long siege.

Although a brilliant defensive strategist, he also knew that sometimes, attack was the best form of defence. Had he not organized the long march that had ended in the surprise attack on Kewatta's supply lines that had effectively ended that war?

Hundreds of carrier pigeons were trained to deliver letters. Parrots were also deployed to transmit secret messages. During the battle, it had been Mahosadha's idea to build ramparts of earth with parapets of stones and debris. He had built watchtowers on elevated vantage points, from where he could spy on the advancing enemy. Moats were dug, deep and wide, which he ordered to be filled not only with water, but with lizards, crocodiles and pythons. Giant catapults were built to propel giant flaming rocks and other deadly armaments into the ranks of their enemies.

He also had hundreds of spies under him, and he sent them out to neighbouring cities. They often brought news of the secret plans of neighbouring kings who bore enmity towards Janaka. And while Mahosadha certainly held Sita's presence in the kingdom to be a blessing, and the bow to be a celestial treasure, he also knew that the kingdom owed its prosperity to the efforts of its ministers, its soldiers and all of its citizens, who had worked tirelessly to rebuild everything they had lost in times of war and drought.

If anything, he felt that the spiritual realm was a greater source of aggravation for the kingdom. Take Tataka for example, and her foul son. Just that morning, Mahosadha had received yet another report that a young sage had been attacked and devoured in the forest. The demons were a constant threat. Neither the sages, who had spiritual might without physical strength, nor the army, which had physical strength without spiritual might, had yet been able to defeat them. If only the king would realize that the problem here was a tactical and logistical one, not a matter of mere prophecies!

His heart heavy and his mind full, Mahosadha continued his wait. When exactly would the king grant him an audience? Was not the prime minister of a kingdom important enough to give priority to? His mind churned as he contemplated the path ahead.

The Secret

Ashtavakra's heart sank momentarily, as a grim thought crossed his mind. A shade of gloom descended on his face, as he assimilated what his grandfather was asking him to do. He was not impressed by Janaka's quest nor did the problems of Mithila concern him. His focus was on the question to which, the answer now seemed close. He asked Uddalaka, 'So, what do you think happened to my father? Mother said there was talk of a debate.'

'People believe that Kahoda was killed because of his failure in the debate with Bandi, the court scholar. The punishment for losing a debate with Bandi was drowning in the river. Six sages had met with the same fate before him.'

'And then?' Ashtavakra and Sujata looked at him with horror and anticipation.

'But that was a story only for the people of the palace and the kingdom. The boat with the seven sages who were meant to be drowned in the river, was actually ferried to the Himalayas.'

'Himalayas?' Ashtavakra asked. 'Why?'

Uddalaka continued, 'Kahoda and the six other sages had been entrusted with a special mission to engage in tapas—a form of deep meditation. It was believed that the peace of the Himalayas would deepen their journey into the infinite, helping them fathom and stir the accumulated spiritual power they all possessed. Their objective was to keep the power of the Asuras away from the kingdom of Mithila.'

Sujata was aghast, 'A penance for fourteen years? Father, how did you come to know about this?' she asked plaintively.

'Sujata, forgive me. I have been waiting for the right time to tell you this. I received a message from Kahoda a long time ago. Because it was an extremely secretive task and related to the kingdom's security, I was instructed to remain silent.'

Uddalaka felt a weight lift from his chest. Sujata's eyes were brimming with tears, and she nodded quietly to her father. Uddalaka continued. 'And, Ashtavakra, the king needs a person like you now. If he does not have the right guidance, he will just be misled by his conniving sages.'

Sujata intervened, 'But how will Ashtavakra do that? What reason will he have to go to the palace? How will he reach out to the king?'

Uddalaka said, 'It is not going to be easy. Ashtavakra has to find a way to do that.' Uddalaka paused, and then said, 'He cannot tell the king that he is the son of Kahoda. Besides, even if he enters the palace, the sages will prevent him from meeting the king. They all know their worth, and when a genuine sage full of wisdom appears, they will sense it. They might employ all manner of tricks to keep Ashtavakra away from the king.'

Ashtavakra smiled wryly, turned towards Uddalaka, and questioned, 'Why do the sages live in the palace? If they are real sages, they don't need a palace. The real seekers are beyond all such luxuries.'

Uddalaka looked at Ashtavakra and thought, while struggling to outgrow the limits of his crooked body; he had also outgrown many things, including tradition. Awe and respect for his grandson overwhelmed him. How had such a young child gained so much wisdom at such an early stage?

Uddalaka ruminated on the circumstances of Ashtavakra's birth. He was born untainted, a prodigy who had learned everything at an early stage of his life. His soul thwarted every layer of identity and sustained its strength to accept everything without judgement. His wisdom was so pure and strong that while still in his mother's womb, upon hearing his father Kahoda chanting a mantra wrongly, Ashtavakra had corrected him.

Kahoda had felt insulted. In anger, when the universe was aligned well to accept the declaration, he cursed his unborn child to be crippled with eight curves. Thus, Ashtavakra was born a cripple, with eight bends in his body, but he remained a pure and wise soul. Uddalaka did not need any more proof. He somehow knew that Ashtavakra's knowledge was sufficient.

Ashtavakra continued. 'Through our individual will, we can excel in anything.'

Delighted, Uddalaka, raised his head high and with wide eyes turned towards Sujata and said, 'I believe your son is grown and mature enough to go to the palace.'

Sujata, still worried about her young, physically challenged son, did not say anything.

Ashtavakra turned to her. 'Mother, I am going to meet the king. And I will bring my father back,' he said with unwavering conviction.

'Oh, Ashtavakra!' She hugged him tightly and sobbed.

'Oh, Mother! Do not weep. I can take care of myself. I want you to know that nothing can limit or surpass the strength of my mind.'

Sujata looked at him and turned towards her father with pleading eyes. 'I have already lost my husband. I have only my son now. I can't part with him as well. I am worried.'

'No, Sujata. You should know who Ashtavakra is. Nothing can stop him. He has not been tainted by the outside world. He was pure even before he came to this earth. He has already made his decision. He is ready to meet the king,' Uddalaka said with finality.

Uddalaka turned towards Ashtavakra and said, 'Very well, then. When are you planning to leave? It's a very long journey from here. You need to cross mountains and rivers. Mount Meru is the tallest peak on the way.'

But Ashtavakra was confident in succeeding in his quest. His mind was already so intent on his mission that he hardly noticed his surroundings anymore. He said distractedly, 'Tomorrow morning, before dawn breaks.'

Meanwhile, on a mountain at the roof of the world, two men sat by a fire lighted in front of a stone dwelling. Looking over the snow-topped peaks, one of them inhaled deeply, and ran his fingers ruminatingly through his snow-white beard. His eyes glimmered with a fire, a spiritual light. He turned his eyes upwards to see a golden eagle circling above them.

'The moment is upon us,' he said to his companion. 'The stars are moving. It will happen soon.'

Ahimsa

Just as Mahosadha was about to lose patience and barge into the king's chamber, the door creaked open. Janaka stepped out, his eyebrows raised in surprise to see Mahosadha waiting for him.

Mahosadha greeted him. 'Maharaj! I must speak to you about two very important matters.'

Janaka fixed a serene gaze on Mahosadha and gestured at him to continue.

'First, I have news from our spies that Sudhanvan is planning an attack.'

Janaka nodded, but his expression remained perfectly calm. 'And the second?'

Mahosadha was taken aback. How could the king be so indifferent to news of an impending attack?

'Maharaj...Is it true that you have ordered cuts to the army?'

'Yes, Mahosadha. Those were my orders.' Janaka's voice was even and unmoved.

'Maharaj! Is this the time to take such a step? Sudhanvan's army is already much better equipped and larger than ours.'

'Mahosadha, we have fought so many wars, against Kewatta, Chulani and many others. We could have avoided those wars had we followed the path of ahimsa, the path of non-violence.'

Mahosadha could not believe what the king had said. He looked at Janaka, lost for words.

'Mahosadha, I have had this in my mind for many years. It is high time to think about choosing a different path; a path to peace, not a path to war.'

'Maharaj! This makes absolutely no sense to me. You know our kingdom's history very well. We have always fought wars of self-defence.'

'But, on most of those occasions, self-defence was only an excuse,' replied Janaka calmly. 'It is true that our forefathers fought wars, and that the Videha kings have a proud history as warriors. But when we learn something new, and when our heart tells us that it is true, we change ourselves to suit that truth.' Mahosadha's mouth fell open but Janaka continued.

'Whenever possible, we need to uphold the highest virtue—and that is ahimsa.

Mahosadha was dumbfounded. He glanced at the guards, expecting some sort of reaction, but they remained stoic; their eyes looking straight ahead. If they paid Janaka's words any heed, they did not let it show.

'Mahosadha,' Janaka went on, 'We need to think about the concept of a just war and engage in reasonable self-defence. When we do mete out punishment, we ensure it is proportionate to the crime.'

Mahosadha couldn't keep the confusion from his face. *Where on earth is all this coming from? Is he under some kind of spell?*

Janaka continued.

'You know, when Sudhanvan was here for the last swayamvar, we had every reason to fight when he drew his sword. But we did not. We upheld the highest virtue. This should be the Videha path, always. And I will maintain this tradition by introducing ahimsa as a new practice. We have to avoid war. We need to engage in sincere and truthful dialogue with each other.'

'Dialogue?' Mahosadha snorted with derision. 'Even with our enemies?'

'Of course. If war is required, its cause must be just. Its purpose should be virtuous, its objective—to restrain the wicked. Its aim should be peace and its methods should be lawful.'

'Maharaj, you have never practised such a philosophy before. Our enemies are already prepared for us, under the impression that we are the best warriors in the world. And if they come and see that we are not prepared, they will not ask why. They will overrun us and kill every man, woman and child. Surely you see that?'

'Mahosadha, this is what you think. With mindsets like yours, you and the others are collectively bringing about war. When two armies face each other, both anticipating war, it takes only a spark to ignite the fire. But can you imagine what would happen if the parties did not have that expectation? Conflicts can always be resolved by dialogue.'

Mahosadha was flabbergasted. 'Only if the two parties are willing to talk! You say I am preoccupied with thoughts of preparation for war...Of course I am! There is an army on its way intending to destroy us. All of us! This is my duty! Are you saying that ahimsa, this new principle, will lead to the end of war—especially when only practised by one side?'

'No, I am not saying that. There will still be wars. But in the event of war, we need to change our strategy. Wars should be fought only to defeat the opponent, not to cause misery to our enemies.'

'But wars bring misery. What you say makes no sense,'

sputtered Mahosadha, his face slightly red now.

'Misery and suffering, like everything else, are a matter of degree. During the war against Kewatta we used arrows smeared with poison, did we not? And crocodiles and snakes in the moats. Arrows, perhaps, are unavoidable, but poison should not be permitted, neither wild animals. We are not savages. Unarmed people should be spared. The wounded should not be killed, but given medical aid. Women, children and civilians must never be injured, under any circumstances.'

Mahosadha exclaimed, 'Maharaj! I truly understand what you are saying. But do you honestly think that our enemies will follow the same principles? To them, victory is victory—no matter how it is achieved.'

'I know that what I am telling you is not easy. Ahimsa requires more strength, and is more responsible than traditional war. We have two responsibilities here: we need to help both the oppressed and the oppressor.'

'Help the oppressor?'

'Mahosadha, the oppressor is not aware that he is acting out of ignorance. So it is our responsibility to make them understand what they are doing is wrong.'

'Sudhanvan carries with him the insult and pain of your prior encounter. And his soldiers are highly motivated, because they believe if they get the bow and Sita, they will have all the power of the world, and their kingdom will flourish with prosperity. And we—on the eve of a battle—are we to step back? This is insane!'

'I have no problem with you preparing the army. But I do not foresee a war,' Janaka replied.

'Maharaj! Please forgive this bluntness, but may I share my honest opinion?'

'Certainly.'

Mahosadha hesitated. Then he spoke, 'People are talking about your overindulgence in spiritual and philosophical matters. Many of them believe you are forgetting your most important duty, which is to protect your land. Ahimsa is a good practice, if we can introduce it gradually. But I don't know how practical it will be for the current situation.' He stopped, looked Janaka in the eye, and continued. 'I believe that the sages are not being helpful. Rather, they are confusing you even further.'

Mahosadha's words were brusque, and he worried for a moment that Janaka would rebuke him. But the king simply listened, his eyes as wide and accepting as they had always been, his mouth set in the same compassionate half-smile.

Mahosadha continued, encouraged by Janaka's passive reaction.

'We can depend upon the counsel of these brahmin sages to a certain extent, but we have to remember that we are kshatriyas, we are warriors and we must take immediate action, using our intuitive sense to act upon things. That—as you know—is how kingdoms survive.'

Janaka granted him an indulgent smile.

'I understand what you say, Mahosadha. But it has always been the Videha tradition to listen to the sages first, before we take any action.'

'I could accept that if the sages knew anything about our current predicament. Do they know that we have fewer elephants and horses than in the past? That the animals we have, lack the experience of war? Are they aware that our younger soldiers have never seen a battle, and they are carrying weapons that belonged to their fathers and grandfathers? And that while our neighbours invest in new training and weaponry and recruits, our investment in defence is to be cut? No, of course, they do not. But I do.'

'Don't worry. I have seen many wars in my life. We have bigger things to worry about,' Janaka replied.

Mahosadha couldn't say anything more; his words choked in his throat. He had not expected this—the talk of ahimsa. He could take no more. He turned to leave. But before walking away, he made one final remark.

'Maharaj, I have tried, but it is obvious to me that I cannot change your mind. I shall, as always, do my best with the resources that are at my disposal. But I fear for you and I fear for the kingdom, for I have heard that not only do you have enemies who approach the gate, but some who are within it.'

Janaka looked at Mahosadha anxiously. This was the first time that he heard his prime minister talk to him this way.

'You need to be very careful who you trust,' said Mahosadha gravely.

'Why do you say that?'

'Because there are people inside the palace, people you trust, who wish harm upon you.'

With that, Mahosadha turned and left.

His mind was not disturbed anymore. He knew what needed to be done.

❋

Janaka frowned. Threats and more threats. Was there no end to them? Mahosadha, much as he respected him, was not a man at peace with himself.

His conversation with the prime minister had drained him. Janaka felt his heart sink once again, a ball of dread forming within his chest. He needed reassurance. He needed to speak to Sita. He stepped out, seeking his daughter.

Unknown to Janaka, Sudhanvan, camping on the borders of Mithila, and possible traitors within the kingdom were not the only threats he faced.

Deep in the forests, creatures were stirring. They had lain dormant for too long. The time has come.

BOOK TWO
SAMSARA

In the limitless ocean of Myself
The winds of the mind
Roil the myriad waves of the world.

2.23 ASHTAVAKRA GITA

The King's Confidante

Janaka stepped into a little garden in the centre of the palace compound and saw Sita speaking to an old man. He recognized him as one of the palace gardeners. It came as no surprise that Sita was listening so intently to the old man. She was the epitome of love, care and empathy. And for the king, his most trusted confidante.

Upon seeing Janaka, the old gardener got up and, bowing to the princess and the king, took his leave. Sita whirled around, surprised to see Janaka there.

'Father! I did not see you come.'

With a rustle of rose-coloured silk, she approached him and bent to touch his feet. Janaka looked down at the lovely young woman.

Her upper garment, edged with gold embroidery, gracefully fell forward on her shoulders and arms as she bent; this young woman had replaced his little girl. He gently pulled her to her feet and gazed into her eyes, while holding her shoulders with both hands, as if he were cradling the most delicate of flowers.

'Father, may I ask a favour of you?'

'Of course, my darling,' replied Janaka.

'Damodar—the gardener—was telling me about his travels in the far south when he was a young man. He told me how the orchids there used to attract hummingbirds, like the sapphire-spangled emerald hummingbird. I was wondering if it would be possible to perhaps plant some orchids in the palace gardens.

I have heard so much about hummingbirds and I have yet to see one.'

Janaka couldn't help but smile.

'Of course, my dearest. I shall have the chief gardener look into it. The palace may soon be home to the sound of tiny flapping wings!'

'Thank you, Father!' Sita exclaimed. It warmed Janaka's heart to see his daughter so happy, at the approval of such a simple request.

Then there was silence and Sita looked away.

'Is there something wrong?' he asked.

'No, nothing, Father,' replied Sita.

'I think I know you well enough to know that is not true, Sita. What ails you?'

'No, no. Nothing at all…Well…' Sita paused and then continued. 'Damodar has a son who lives in Kosala and he is fearful for him. Apparently there is talk of war…'

'Come, sit with me,' Janaka said quietly, indicating the low wall around the fountain. 'You are correct, as usual. Right now, Kosala is torn. King Dasharatha is sick. And Ravana, the Asura king from Lanka, threatens Ayodhya.'

Sita's heart sank. The look on her face did not escape Janaka's attention.

'Sita, the swayamvar is fast approaching. You know that whoever wins the test will receive your hand in marriage.'

'Father, I am aware of it.'

'Are you unhappy with the way the swayamvar is being conducted?' Janaka asked.

'Have I ever objected to any of your decisions, Father?'

'I know you have not. I was hoping that someone suitable would compete.'

'But Father, what worries me is that I am becoming a burden to all of you.'

Her eyes were mysterious and deep brown, with thick eyelashes that were now very moist, and utterly unable to disguise any feelings she might have. The sun beat down directly into the walled garden. Her tightly coiled black hair gleamed. She met her father's gaze with questioning eyes.

'I know why this is affecting you—the little birds around here are not the only ones who sing.'

Sita looked at him with even greater interest.

'I know you have someone in mind; someone like Rama, the prince of Ayodhya. If that happens, it will be a good match for all of us. Rama's father Dasharatha is the only king with whom we have a solid friendship. But the path before us is unclear. If Rama is to win you in marriage, he has to come and take the test. I know that this relationship would have been ideal for all of us, but the timing does not look auspicious.'

Sita sat in silence. Her heart sank further hearing her father say this. But she tried not to show it, for she was acutely aware of all the problems that were currently assailing her father.

'However,' continued Janaka, 'Some of my advisers have counselled me to send a part of our army in support of Dasharatha, since there is a threat of an attack from Ravana. If we are victorious, certain opportunities for bringing the two kingdoms closer would certainly open up.'

Sita nodded hopefully.

'All our fates are intertwined, my dear daughter. If what I hear about Ravana is true, then the course of all our fates may soon become different. I may have to go to war, and that troubles me.'

'Oh, Father! You have battled evil before and have always emerged victorious.'

'But I am tired now. I have seen too much war. I want to bring an end to war, not wage it. I want to become a true Videha, but it seems like life will not allow it.'

Janaka regarded his daughter as his equal in every sphere and often consulted her on palace affairs. She would listen to everything with a depth of understanding that rivalled that of Satananda. She often travelled with him on official affairs. She offered solutions to every problem. It was a magical skill, Janaka thought. He could discuss any matter on Earth with her.

'No one person can end war, Father,' said Sita gently. 'There will be no peace on Earth until there is peace in the heart of every man.'

'This is a great truth, Sita, and all I can do until that moment arrives is to try and align myself and this kingdom to that truth—however long it takes.' He paused. 'There is something else though.'

'Tell me, Father.'

'Sita, my dear daughter, I don't understand what is happening to me.'

Sita looked at Janaka waiting for him to tell her more.

Janaka continued, 'The dream has shaken me to my very core. It had made me question who I actually am, and since then, I have gone deeper within myself in order to find the answer. But the soul will not accept a violent man. In order to go deeper, I must make peace with myself. But how can I do that when my role as a king involves war and struggle and death? There is no escaping it. For many years now, I have been thinking of bringing the culture of ahimsa into the affairs of the kingdom. But how can I do that? How can I prevent other kings from coveting you and the bow and our prosperity? The wise ones say that the dream is a warning, as I have had it twice now in a relatively short Span of time. But a warning of what?'

He stopped to take a breath, and then continued, 'It's probably a call for me to seek life beyond what we experience, to remind me about the meaninglessness of the temporal world. But do I know what the dream portends? Or if it means anything at all?'

Janaka looked at Sita as if he was expecting an answer, but she did not reply. It was as if she needed to hear more.

'But people do not care about such matters. They have their own problems. They think: *How can a Videha king who has so many enemies promote such a doctrine of peace? All he has to do is find a balance between the inner and the outer.* I have done that for years. But now—since the dream—I believe things have been thrown out of balance. I am at war with myself.'

There was another pause. This time, Sita did reply. 'Oh, Father! You've forgotten. You've told me many times that life is like this. That we are in the midst of never-ending challenges, and that they are inevitable, because they are the results of our choices. And the bigger the challenge, the bigger the test. You also taught me this: if something like this happens, it is proof that we are destined for a larger purpose. The important thing is not the struggle, nor the winning or losing, but that in every stage in our life, our soul evolves and grows spiritually.'

'But Sita, as a king, how do I practice non-violence? At the same time, how can I secure our borders? This is the legacy I want to leave behind.'

'You question your ability to be a true Videha,' said Sita. 'But you have the answer. You know it already.' Her voice was calm and soothing.

'I am sure I do not, my daughter. We spend our wealth on defence, and the soldiers and generals train for war and get paid—as do those that forge the spears and those that cut the arrows. They all become accustomed to the idea of war, so much so that they begin to yearn for it. So, we all wait for news of aggression from others, and we jump at the chance to start preparing. Sometimes, the enemies come to know that we are preparing for a possible threat. So they start preparing their artillery. Rumours spread between both groups, and any minor squabble will precipitate the reasons for war. We have become accustomed to these habits and we must break them! Somewhere in my mind, something is telling me that this is possible.'

'There, you just said it. You do know the answer! Break these patterns, Father! Do what you feel is right for you. But please remain silent about this for now; if you discuss this with anyone, you might not recieve any support.'

Sita continued, 'Father, you have a solution. You know it already. Someone will come to advise you, I am sure. You will soon realize it on your own. A sage will soon come to give you the knowledge you are seeking.'

Janaka sighed with relief. He knew the truth of Sita's words. They sat, not speaking.

Then he said, 'I will act upon the idea of ahimsa. This is how I will maintain the Videha tradition, and how I will do my dharma, my duties as a king. When I am done, I need to leave the kingdom in your younger brother's hands. When my father gave me the responsibility of this kingdom, I was very young. I want to ensure that when the time comes for Bhanumat to take his place on the throne, he is ready for Mithila, and Mithila is ready for him.'

'It will be Father, it will be.'

Those words, to him, felt like a prophecy.

Janaka looked at Sita. Would this precious girl ever know how important her words were to him?

In another part of the palace, hidden from view, one of the king's sages held out his hand and from the shadows, another hand emerged. Something was passed between the two. As the sage turned to leave, he tucked a pouch into his waist, and covered it with his upper garment so that it was hidden. The sage had a satisfied smirk on his face.

Preparations

If joy could be a place, then on the eve of the swayamvar, it would be called Mithila.

Kushadwaja was as good as his word. Without any help from Janaka, he had ensured Mithila wore the air of a carnival. Thanks to him, the entire kingdom's affluence was on display. As the day drew near, the whole city was festooned with decorations and bunting. Vivid banners, painted with the likeness of mythical animals, were on display in the streets of Mithila. It looked like every building and monument was bedecked with flowers, a light breeze making the whole city look like a rippling field of bright colour and joy.

From the Nandivandana Courtyard to the palace gate, there were gambling tables, dancing girls, cockfights, snake charmers, sword swallowers, bullfights and clowns with painted faces. Dice players competed enthusiastically and people thronged in groups to watch; heads craning to catch a glimpse of the game in progress. Laughter and screams came in festive bursts from the joyously assembled groups. The palace kitchens were in a frenzy of activity and the aroma of delicious food wafted through the air. Villagers from different parts of Mithila trickled into the city. Men, women and children were wonderstruck at all the sights. The whole city rejoiced, waiting to welcome the princes and kings who would try their hand at stringing the divine bow. Giant gongs were struck and their reverberations resonated through the streets in waves. Occasionally, entertainers blew conches to announce the intervals of each form of entertainment.

In the hall where the bow lay, Janaka surveyed the audience around him. Prayers were being chanted, for this was where the swayamvar would take place. But Janaka was restless. He was still haunted by the message he had received at the yagna. Though many of those around him were close to him, he would not confide in them about his anxieties for fear that it might spoil their mood and ruin the occasion.

In the right corner of the hall sat Sita and her cousins Mandavi and Srutakirti, elegantly dressed. Mandavi and Srutakirti were quietly teasing Sita, whose dark eyes looked like those of a doe. Her garments were rich and ornate, beautifully embellished as befitting a bride. Her neck was adorned with exquisite jewellery, her arms with pearl bangles, and her ankles with jingling bells. Her diamond earrings sparkled like the brightest stars, lighting up her beautiful face.

After the prayers, Janaka raised his head and addressed the gathered crowd.

'I welcome you all to this wonderful occasion. Let us give thanks for the happy position that Mithila now finds itself in. Do you understand how Mithila has managed to flourish with such prosperity, when all of our neighbours are facing droughts, shortages and other difficult times?'

The assembly, comprising of the royal family, courtiers and important city officials, listened attentively to their king. 'It is because of two miracles. The first is the power of Shiva's bow, and the second is our illustrious Sita, the miracle that emerged from the earth as a gift from the divine. Let us hope that providence will grant us a third miracle: a husband for Sita tomorrow!'

With that, the crowd cheered and the festivities resumed.

Janaka sat down, internally quiet as the people cheered around him. It had been two years since the sages had pronounced the man to marry Sita would have to lift the magical bow of Shiva and string it. Since the time of Devarata, each one of Janaka's forefathers, the Videha kings had been the custodians of the magical bow. It had lain for centuries in the palace's great hall, awaiting the hand that would be its master.

It was during Devarata's time that the bow had been hurled from heaven. The whole kingdom had been lit up one dark night by a sudden flash of lightning that had appeared a thousand times brighter than anything anyone had seen before. It was accompanied by a thunderous roar that seemed to shake the whole world. It occurred after the time when the Asuras, the demons, having taken over the three revolving aerial cities, had wreaked havoc in the universe. All hope seemed lost until the sages of the earth approached Shiva for help. In response, Shiva created the great bow and an arrow. The demon cities were felled by a single shot, in what came to be known as the Tripura Samhara. This celestial conflagration then cleansed the earth, air and sky of all Asuras. But the bow's special power did not dissipate and remained within it, silently dormant, right up to the present day. Mithila had since been invaded many times by neighbouring kings, but it was believed that it was protected from its enemies by a divine power. Although the bow lay motionless, it hummed with a strange force that made it impossible to lift, let alone string.

So, it was right that whoever could carry out this task would have to possess attributes of the divine to win the hand of Sita, who was also divine.

The hall was circular with a domed roof. In the middle

stood an enormously long table covered with a red silk cloth, trimmed in gold. It was on this that the bow lay. It gleamed in the morning sunlight that passed through the crystal dome of the hall. Around the table, fresh flowers lay strewn, emphasizing the stark, lean violence of the weapon in the centre. The bow was sturdy, and much larger than a normal bow—as wide as a man's arm at its thickest part.

All the people gathered in the hall looked at the bow with their palms joined, and bowed their heads in reverence. Occasionally, some chanted holy mantras. Swirls of burning incense rose in the air, the aroma slowly filling the room. Janaka approached the giant table, picked up some flowers from a basket and threw them on the bow with great veneration.

Janaka turned towards Kushadwaja and smiled at him appraisingly. *Yes,* he told himself, *My brother has done everything he could to make this event as beautiful as it can be.*

The occasional beating of drums could be heard from outside the palace, in the Nandivandana Courtyard, and bursts of laughter could be heard from the dice players.

'Kushadwaja!' Janaka called out. 'You have organized everything so well. Can we assume that we are going to have enough participants tomorrow?'

'Brother, are you still not sure that the swayamvar is going to be a success?' replied a slightly annoyed Kushadwaja.

'You have made an auspicious start,' said Janaka. An uncomfortable silence fell between them and lingered, till Satananda interrupted.

'Kushadwaja, your brother only worries because the signs are not very favourable for us,' Satananda said authoritatively, his facial expression heavy with forewarning.

'I have done what I could,' said Kushadwaja. 'Mahosadha

has confirmed that all the invitations have been accepted. But I still need your opinion regarding the preparations against Sudhanvan.'

This was the last thing that Janaka wanted to hear. He hoped the subject would be dropped, but then Satananda joined in.

'Maharaj! I also think we have to do something about it. We have to be very careful.'

The other sages nodded their heads in unison. Satananda glanced at Janaka, stroking his beard. He opened his mouth as though to say something, but Kushadwaja interrupted.

'After the events of last year, Sudhanvan might do anything to stop the other princes and kings from coming to Mithila. Accordingly, I have asked Mahosadha to increase security at the borders. In addition, I have asked elite soldiers be stationed around the city and disguised as commoners in the streets. We are monitoring the entire palace for threats.'

An odd look came over Janaka's face. 'But,' Kushadwaja said, tripping over his words as if in a hurry to get them out. 'I have taken special care at the borders.'

Janaka squinted at Kushadwaja. 'But I have already given the responsibility of security—at the border and the palace— to Mahosadha, as it requires the utmost discretion and experience. Have you also been involved with that?' I don't think you need to do anything now regarding the preparation against Sudhanvan. Let Mahosadha take care of it. He is more experienced in matters regarding the security of the kingdom. Recently, Mahosadha had camped at the border for days. He had even visited some other small neighbouring countries to make preparations for the protection of Mithila.'

Kushadwaja clenched his jaw, supressing the anger that rose in response to the king's indifference.

He fought to keep his voice calm and level. 'I was also part of every preparation for border protection. It was my decision to send a few hand-picked spies into the countryside.'

Janaka did not fully understand Kushadwaja's annoyance, and a look of confusion crept onto his face. He furrowed his brow.

'Why would you do such a thing?' Janaka asked tersely. 'That's not your responsibility. Mahosadha is taking care of security. You did not have to act on things I did not ask you to do. I have only told you to organize the swayamvar.'

Kushadwaja clenched his fist. He knew that the incident that had occurred during the war against Kewatta still lingered in his brother's mind.

Three years ago during the war with Kewatta, Kushadwaja had been positioned on Daranya Mountain, instructed to look out for approaching enemies. After many hours of waiting, he grew impatient and began to suspect that he'd been purposefully kept from the battlefield. He made a hasty decision to go back and join the others, leaving his post unwatched. Unbeknown to him, Kewatta's army was at that moment marching its way to Mithila through the Daranya Mountain. It was not long after he came back to the base of the mountain, where Mithila's army was, that the enemy stealthily attacked. Only prime minister Mahosadha's intervention and quick strategy saved Mithila's army from being defeated. However, more than two hundred soldiers had perished. The king mourned the loss of his men for years, and Kushadwaja had carried the burden of guilt in his heart.

'I don't understand why Mahosadha did not tell you about my role in border protection if it was against your wishes. This really is news to me.' Kushadwaja said.

Once again, Kushadwaja had tried to do his best for the kingdom, and once again, he had been humiliated by his brother—this time publicly. His mood began to darken as he considered his options. He knew now—beyond all previous doubt—that he needed allies within the palace who had the ears of the king.

Swayamvar

When Janaka woke up the next morning, it was with the thought that he was about to lose his beloved Sita. She was the only person who understood him well, and although he knew that he was blessed with her presence for at least this final day, he was also grieved to think that he may well not have her to confide in, tomorrow.

He overcame this gloomy notion though and roused himself from his bed quickly. It was the day of the swayamvar and duty called. He dressed without assistance, eager to see how many kings and princes had lined up for the contest to win Sita's hand. Everyone wanted Sita for their own. The swayamvar had been organized a couple of times before, but no one had been able to win her. It was things like this that made people wonder why destiny was being so unkind to Sita. But every silver lining carries a dark cloud, Janaka rationalized, and hurried from his bedroom to the great hall.

There was something off about the palace today, though—something that did not sit quite right in the king's mind. It struck him only as he was approaching the vast doors, along the colonnade of windows: the morning seemed quiet, too quiet.

The doors to the great hall flew open and Mahosadha rushed forth, wringing his hands with a worried look on his face. 'Maharaj!' he cried, 'No one is here for the swayamvar. Where have we gone wrong?'

Janaka pushed the doors open again and strode into the hall—it was indeed empty, except for Kushadwaja and a few servants, who were all gathered at the balcony to gaze across the city.

Raising his voice, Janaka directed his reply across the expanse, so that his brother would hear him. 'I gave complete responsibility for this contest, including the invitations, to Kushadwaja. Perhaps you should ask him.'

Everyone turned towards Kushadwaja. His broad, handsome face was distraught and defensive. 'I have done the best I could, within my limits. Scores of messengers have gone out to more than one hundred kingdoms. And Mahosadha confirmed it. I cannot explain it, Brother.'

Janaka stood stone-like, his eyes fixed on a point beyond the balcony railing. The sky was clouded and the trees outside the garden were still, with no breeze to pamper them. The roads leading to and from the palace in every direction were empty, filled only with the music of hopeful performers and the concerned murmurs of the townspeople.

At last, he turned to Mahosadha, 'You had confirmed that all we had invited had accepted to come. Then there is nothing to worry about. Let us hope that our guests will be here by this afternoon.'

※

King Janaka, Queen Sunayana, their daughters, nieces, Chandrabagha and their maids, had all gathered near the bow in the palace hall. Even among the high-born women, the illustrious Sita shone like a jewel. Her sister Urmila and her cousins, Mandavi and Srutakirti, were clinging to her, as always. She emerged from their ranks with her head bowed, to sit close to the man she knew as her father. She was dressed in sea-blue silk; flowers were woven into her braid, and diamonds had been placed in her ears. Within this closed chamber, the sounds of merriment and jubilation were distant, as if pushed far away by the thick atmosphere of concern.

Afternoon arrived. Janaka, Mahosadha, the sages and many courtiers gathered in the palace hall. Outside the palace, hundreds of performers were assembled, ready to add beauty to the celebration—magicians, dancers, jugglers, snake charmers and hundreds of serving girls. The hall's tables were laden with food and fruits. Mahosadha leaned close to whisper in the king's ear.

'Maharaj! Still, there is no one. The crowd grows outside the palace. They sense that something is wrong and are becoming restless. You must do or say something.'

Janaka turned to him, 'Did you give us the wrong information Mahosadha? How did this happen?'

Satananda interrupted, before Mahosadha could reply.

'This is definitely not a good sign, my Lord. The first ill omen was your dream, and the second is this absence of guests.' His voice trembled with fear, and the king briefly remembered his wife's belief that these men were incompetent. Maybe she was right, as was Mahosadha.

Janaka shot a dark look at Satananda, not liking what he heard.

Suddenly there was a murmuring outside the palace. Everybody turned towards the balcony that opened to the front yard. Had the guests come at last? Perhaps they had simply lost their way, and all of them had finally arrived together. Of course, that was absurd—all the kings and princes knew their way to Mithila's palace, unless they had been attacked by

Tataka or one of the other demons in the forest, and the king did not want to believe this was true. Janaka strode towards the balcony and opened the door. To his surprise, he saw a crowd of people in the yard.

The front yard of the palace was packed from end to end and the Nandivandana Courtyard, the wide road that extended across the foreyard of the palace, was teeming with people. Ordinary citizens and aristocrats alike thronged the square. More were arriving on foot, and a few of them were on horseback. Immediately, a squad of the king's soldiers took defensive positions around the gravelled, circular yard.

'Long live the king!' the people shouted. Janaka waved his hands and smiled at them.

One of them shouted, 'O Maharaj! What is happening to Mithila? Why is nobody here for the swayamvar?'

Raising his voice to be heard, Janaka replied, 'There is nothing to worry about. The invitees will soon be here. Everything is taken care of. Go back to your homes and await the announcement.'

They all stared at the king, dissatisfaction etched upon their faces. No one moved.

'I said, everything will be taken care of,' Janaka announced once more. 'So, for the time being, all of you can go home. I command you.'

The king had to be obeyed. Everybody turned and began to return home in small groups, some of them grumbling. They hung their heads in disappointment.

Janaka turned back to Mahosadha and said, 'Get me Kushadwaja immediately. He has a lot to answer for!' His voice rang, and he experienced a flash of pure, white-hot anger, as if his head would burst with its intensity.

Mahosadha exchanged a glance with his soldiers. 'Maharaj... Kushadwaja has not been seen in the palace since morning.'

'How can this be? Where did he go?' Janaka asked.

'I have asked. No one knows.'

Janaka shook his head, fire blazing in his eyes. 'And you, Mahosadha! You confirmed to Kushadwaja that all had accepted our invitation. Where did you go wrong?'

Mahosadha did not meet his eyes. Head bowed, he said, 'Maharaj! I had warned you that Sudhanvan was preparing for an attack. Perhaps it's his doing. I will send our men out to see what went wrong.'

✻

Dusk was falling, and still no guests arrived. The sun in the west stained the sky vermilion, disappearing into the hills and briefly silhouetting the bulls as they returned to their barns. The birds sitting on the palace dome chirped, crows cawed as they flew to their nests. Darkness was approaching like an uninvited guest. The oil lamps flung flickering shadows against the stone walls.

Only Sita and the king remained, sitting next to each other in front of the bow. Sita seemed more thoughtful than distressed. She lowered her head to look at her hands folded neatly into her lap. Although there were mere inches between them, Janaka felt as if he was on the other side of a great divide. He wanted to speak, but felt unable to get words out. Where was this distance coming from? For the first time in his life, he was unable to talk to his own beloved daughter. It was Sita who broke the silence.

'Father, please,' she said, her voice quiet and resigned. 'There is no need to worry. You can dismiss me for the night.

Nothing good can come of sitting here, allowing fear to beget fear. We will talk later.'

Janaka could not tell if she was trying to minimize his own distress, or if she was sincere. As always, her gentle heart was mysterious to him. She was wise for her age—divine, as the sages had foretold. And indeed, as Janaka thought of his courtiers, of the others who had gathered with them in the hall, he could feel their combined distress resounding throughout the palace, and their quivering doubt about the future. It was the same as it had been twenty years ago, in the worst days of the drought. Fear was contagious. He could not purify his heart of it, and suddenly he could not stand the thought of seeing it mirrored a hundred times on his courtiers' faces.

'Forgive me, Sita,' were the only words he could muster as he kissed her on the temple and bid her goodnight. Then he sat on the floor and buried his face in his hands.

He was alone, except for the animals and demons in the tapestries that hung from the walls. The fearsome lions carved on the pillars, seemed to snarl in the darkness.

He was engrossed in his thoughts, like a man entangled in a forest of doubt. Today had been a disaster. *Something is definitely happening*, he thought. These manifestations were very bad signs and the dream could be a portent of a forthcoming event, the will of god, and the kingdom's inevitable destiny. *What roles do we human beings play when it comes to controlling our fates?* Janaka felt helpless, like an impoverished commoner, caught up in the labyrinth of samsara—the inevitable struggle of mundane life.

Just then, one of the guards slipped into the room and bowed hurriedly, eager to speak.

'Maharaj! Mahosadha is waiting outside to speak with you.'

Janaka frowned. Why would Mahosadha come now? It made no sense for him to seek an audience so soon after being dismissed, unless there was some emergency.

Janaka gestured. 'Let him in.'

Mahosadha entered the room and bowed. 'Maharaj!' he exclaimed, 'I am afraid there is more bad news.'

Janaka rose from the floor as if he had been waiting for it. Sometimes, the heart tells us what is going to happen next, and it then happens. Even as he had been struggling to conquer his anxiety, something else was coming. He had felt it, and he was ready.

'Yes, Mahosadha. I know. Tell me, what is the news?'

'Our spies from the north have just ridden in. They say that Sudhanvan is already on his way to attack Mithila. He has joined forces with the other kingdoms that were slighted last year. It was he who blocked the suitors who were on their way to Mithila for the swayamvar, and he has convinced them to form an alliance. He has his eyes on Sita and the divine bow.'

Janaka looked at his prime minister, trying to hide the expression of disappointment and fatigue that threatened to creep onto his face. He was not ready for another war. He thought of the roomful of frightened faces he had seen just an hour ago, and of Sita's words—*fear begets fear*. He fought to regain his equanimity, and to deliver his reply with a calm smile.

'Mahosadha, keep this to yourself,' he said, suddenly becoming decisive. 'It will only create a panic. Just inform Senapati Mahadev, and order him to be prepared for further orders.'

Mahosadha gaped at him. 'Your majesty, this is not something we can ignore. If we don't act on this as soon as possible, things will move beyond our control. We must mobilize our troops.'

'You have your orders. We do nothing yet.'

❋

After Mahosadha left the chamber, Janaka's confidence wavered. Had he not dreamt about Mithila being attacked? Surely it was a premonition of forthcoming calamities and imminent war? The universe has its own way of communicating about the future, and perhaps he was a fool to ignore it.

Janaka felt as if his heart was breaking into pieces; he felt his energy drain from his body, and an uneasiness passed through him. He looked outside the window. The sky was still dark and cloudy, with the threat of rain looming.

The thicket of woods outside the palace stood dark and still, the giant oak and banyan trees ghostly silhouettes against the background of the clouded sky. For a moment, Janaka was shocked to realize what had been inside his mind was outside now. There was nothing to be done but await the imminent storm.

He wanted to meditate, but how could such a troubled mind become calm enough to find stillness?

Janaka then thought back to his old teachers and ancestors. He began calling them in his head, desperately shouting for guidance. He recalled what his teacher, Sage Yajnawalkya, had told him.

'When everything in the world fails to support you, and when nobody is around to speak to you, you must depend on the illumination that comes from within. Only then will you realize that your Self is your light, and your Self your strength, and that there is nothing except your Self when everything else in the world fails.'

Janaka closed his eyes for a moment. He went deep within

himself, and deliberately delved into the pain of his fall into the pit. At first, it was excruciating and terrifying, but then he surrendered himself to the pain, not flinching, not fighting, but accepting. And oddly, the more he accepted it, the less it hurt. Soon, he stopped resisting and the pain disappeared, replaced by a sensation that subsumed his inner world. He realized that when he had consciously accepted the pain, it disappeared.

It was as if a stream was flowing calmly inside him. Where there had been confusion, now there was clarity. Where there was war, now there was peace. Where once there was weakness, now there was strength. He had conquered the beast.

The Arrogant King

The swayamvar, Sita's marriage contest, had been organized twice before, and both times, hundreds of would-be suitors from different parts of the world had flocked to the palace to participate. Last year, a number of them had come many days before the swayamvar and had camped out in the city's streets. Each of them had their fantasies, not only of the beautiful Sita, but of the prosperity that she would surely bring to their kingdom upon marriage.

One of the most eager kings was Sudhanvan. No one—not the citizens of Mithila and certainly not his rival kings and princes—would forget his arrival for the swayamvar the previous year. As people gathered at the gate of Mithila, a roar shook the city walls and all fell silent, heads turning to take in the impressive view of a column of mounted soldiers in glittering silver and black. At its head, astride an elephant, rode the mighty king himself, decked in gold and gems, emanating an air of dark, determined strength. Sudhanvan was one of the most powerful kings in the region, with thousands of men in his army. His reputation was well-known. He had won many wars, annexed many kingdoms and beheaded their rulers, apparently without a second thought.

During the swayamvar last year, he had stood up in the assembly hall and faced the entire gallery of participants.

He had exuded an aura of arrogance and confidence

that rippled outwards across the assembly, in waves of fear and intimidation. Sudhanvan had gazed at them, as if asking, 'Why are you even bothering to compete with me?' He had raised his hands high, rolled his eyes expressively, and twirled his moustache between the tips of his fingers. The kings and princes had sunk into their seats, hushed by the ominous authority of his presence. The assembly hall was filled from wall to wall with Sudhanvan's booming voice.

'Today, I come to take both the bow and Sita! I dare anyone to try and stop me!' He had roared.

Then he had let out a victorious laugh. The assembly fell silent. The king's sages had looked at each other in astonishment.

'I could have come here long before with my troops and taken both Sita and the bow by force. But I believe in peace, and have thus accepted the kind invitation of King Janaka. I am a respectful man.'

He then strode to the giant table placed on a raised platform, on which the bow rested.

He had bent towards it, seized it in his right hand, and attempted to lift it. But he could not. Hushed mutterings arose from the audience and hundreds of women at the back of the assembly hall craned their heads to get a glimpse of the scene. Sudhanvan squared his shoulders, preparing himself again, and this time, wrapped both of his hands around the bow. He endeavoured to lift it with all his might, but the only thing that changed was his face, which turned a deep maroon. His veins bulged out of his forearms and perspiration began to drip copiously from his brow.

Sudhanvan mustered up all his strength and gave one final, impressive tug at the bow. But this time, he lost his balance and was thrown back with what looked like a divine dismissal from the bow. He tumbled down the dais and went sprawling on the floor, looking quite foolish. The whole audience burst into peals of laughter, and Sudhanvan looked around shamefacedly, like a lion that had let its prey go. He rose to his feet, his face now purple with embarrassment and anger.

'Why are you laughing you fools? You have no idea what is happening here! Can you not see that this is a trick? Are you all blind? King Janaka has no intention of allowing any of us to wed his daughter. That is the truth of what is happening here!' His face was dark with rage.

The entire audience fell silent.

'This bow test is a deception! Staged because he wants to deceive the world into thinking he wishes to marry his daughter off. But in reality, he is afraid of losing her and the bow. He knows that his kingdom would not survive without the bow and Sita!'

The crowd was divided, but many of the kings and princes felt some kind of plausibility in his words and started standing up, beginning to shout at Janaka: 'Cheat! Cheat!'

Then Sudhanvan shouted over them,

'Janaka has brought all of us to his palace to make fools of us!'

Sudhanvan withdrew his sword from its sheath and his companions did the same. But the palace guards had already taken out their swords, ready to defend the king.

Then Janaka stepped forward, putting up his hands.

'Stop! We are not here to shed any blood! This is not our tradition. We have guests here today, and it is our duty to protect them.'

Sudhanvan turned to Janaka, and spoke with a swagger.

'Janaka. Count on this. I will show you who I am. You have

deceived a renowned king and you will see that those who have been insulted today will band together against you.' Sudhanvan struggled visibly to control his emotions, still quivering with rage, eager to strike somebody with his unsheathed sword.

It was Senapati Mahadev who came forward to diffuse the situation. 'The Maharaja does not believe in undue violence, and this is the virtue of a Videha king. If you fail to respect Maharaja Janaka's desire for peace, and if you mistake it for weakness, rest assured, you will not return to your kingdom.'

Sudhanvan grunted, obviously unmoved by Mahadev's words. He turned towards the gallery and shouted, 'Do you still want to stay here, fools? Or, do you also want to leave and seek compensation for this insult?'

Many of those present began to shout their support. Sudhanvan puffed up, his face gleaming.

'At least let us protect our honour!' he boomed, before sheathing his sword and storming out of the room, followed by scores of other kings and princes.

Recollecting this incident, King Janaka also remembered his dream—or was it a nightmare? Everything was hanging in the balance. Sudhanvan's lust for power could easily lead to the dream's fulfilment. Yes, the palace could be burnt to the ground, he could be captured and be forced to beg for his life, with all those he loved killed, or violated all around him. On the other hand, he was not without his own resources, one of which was the fertile ground he had been raised on. The Videha tradition of his ancestors ran rich in his veins and gave him courage for the coming confrontation. He felt no fear. However, the reckoning was approaching. Would his dream prove to be true or false? Time would soon tell, but the balance of power was changing.

At the border, meanwhile, Sudhanvan was receiving emissaries and secret couriers, one of whom was from Janaka's own palace. As Sudhanvan's grievance grew, so did his power...

The Queen's Plight

Sunayana entered Janaka's chamber and approached the bedside table with a glass of milk on a silver salver. She placed the milk—which had been mixed with ground almonds and crushed cardamom—on the table. Gloom gave her a stooped gait and she placed the salver on the table slightly more aggressively than was necessary, as if she wanted to grab Janaka's attention. He looked up at her.

'Why do you look so worried and distressed?' Janaka asked Sunayana.

She looked at him without speaking. Her silky hair was tied back in a loose braid, and she was dressed for bed. But something in her eyes hinted at a nervous energy, a lingering worry that had been eating away at her since afternoon.

She started speaking, reluctantly at first.

'Sita brings luck to everyone around her, but she does not bring luck to herself, or to her close relatives.'

Sunayana stood still for some time after she had spoken and looked at Janaka sharply, as if to emphasize what she had said was important and demanded an honest, thoughtful answer.

'I cannot disagree with you,' Janaka answered sincerely. Sunayana had never been anything but a loving, kind mother to Sita. Still, he could not help but remember the joy in her eyes when her own biological children were born—much like the joy he had felt when Sita came to him during the drought.

The thought distressed him slightly.

'How can I say anything unkind about Sita?' Sunayana continued. 'She has brought so many blessings to Mithila. But I do believe that within every blessing, the seed of an equally strong curse may sit. Perhaps you should find out more about the nature of these forces, and do something to ward off potential calamities.'

'Sunayana! Sita has been nothing but a blessing for us all. Your mind is overwrought—you are looking for reasons to be unhappy. Such thoughts will make you unreasonable.' He could not keep the curtness from his voice, despite knowing that this was the root of all their arguments lately.

Sunayana, unhappy with this assessment, retorted, 'I have just shown you a different side of the problem, which you may not see. But now, the fault has become mine. You say that I am the one creating problems.' Her tone rose.

Rolling the end of her sari between her left thumb and forefinger, she continued, 'It is not that I want Sita to leave. It is just that I think that you do not.'

'What do you mean? I know that she must be married. But we cannot intervene with anything that is destined to happen. It is true that there were no suitors at the swayamvar today, but that does not mean that we lose all hope. We need to wait. Time will change everything.'

There was complete silence. There was no noise except for the rustling of the curtains as they billowed in the breeze. Sunayana pinched the bridge of her fine, straight nose.

'Perhaps all of these unwanted events are happening because she does not have a horoscope,' Sunayana muttered under her breath.

❋

Every girl's destiny was inscribed somewhere, and written in that horoscope should be a match—the boy who was fated to marry her. This was an unbreakable universal law, but how could it possibly apply to Sita? Could she even have a horoscope? When she was found in the furrow, she was already perhaps a few weeks old. And nobody had bothered to think about it, for they were all so jubilant about the end of the drought.

Much later, a few years ago, the king had gathered his sages and all of the kingdom's most learned men, hoping that one of them would have the answer to charting Sita's horoscope. Many sages were brought in from the forests to predict Sita's future, but all of them failed. That's when the assembly decided that they would pray in unison, seeking an answer from the Divine.

Suddenly, Satananda rose from his position, as if he had been pushed by a divine hand and started walking up and down the ranks of observers. His gaze grew distant, as if staring at something that no one else could see. Then, within an instant, it seemed that every emotion in existence flashed upon his face. He stopped for a while, seemingly calm, but then stormed from the room, walking as fast as he could through the corridors of the palace. The courtiers and other sages moved to follow him, but the king signalled to them, ordering them to stay where they were. Only King Janaka went after him. Satananda broke into a run, but his steps were steady and decisive, focused on his destination. At last, he entered the hall where the bow was kept. He approached the bow, looked at it, and then stooped for a while to inspect it carefully. He then stood up in silence, a strange sense of relief apparent in his posture, like that of a traveller arriving at his destination after many days of travel, or like that of a fisherman finally feeling the pull of a trapped fish in his net.

Janaka followed Satananda and stood by him, watching as his expression changed from a strange, distant one to a calm, serene smile. Janaka asked Satananda in a low tone, 'What has happened?'

It was then that Satananda made his proclamation. 'Sita is divine,' he said. 'And there is a divine way of solving the problem related to her marriage.' He sighed heavily. 'Whoever strings the bow will be eligible to marry her,' he finished triumphantly, delivering a clear answer to the king's problem. There was joy and merriment in the palace, and the new challenge was announced across the world.

✶

Sunayana edged closer to him and gently placed her hand on his shoulder. 'You know that people are already saying you do not want her to be wed? They are saying that you fear if she leaves, all of Mithila's prosperity will go with her.'

'You are half-right. I do fear her leaving, but as a father—not as a king.' He shook his head in melancholy. 'The sages say I must have her married and I know it to be true.'

Sunayana hesitated as if summoning up the courage to say something. 'I do not trust any of your sages. They are just securing themselves, coming to you with their palms open to receive bountiful gifts. If they were real sages, they would not stay here with you. I am not the only one who feels this way. Why tie our daughter's happiness to a mystical bow, when there are many princes who would be glad to marry her?'

Janaka shook his head. He knew that Satananda had been right about Sita being divine—and believed that he must surely be right about the bow and the marriage as well.

'What we did the past two years for the swayamvar was

different. We used to have a special day for the test. However, I will now declare the bow test open to any participant at any point of time. I am sure the right person will come at the right time.'

'But who will come? How long are we going to wait like this? What about Srutakirti, Mandavi and Urmila? Is our other daughter and our nieces to also wait like this for an indefinite period? They will grow old waiting for Sita to be married.'

'As I told you, we need to be patient.'

'But I do not know if you are going to be with us for such a long time.'

Janaka looked at Sunayana in astonishment.

'What do you mean?'

'These days, aside from all these things happening in the palace, I see that you are battling a host of other problems, problems which we do not understand...or you will not allow us to understand. You are always brooding over things, and I am worried that you will abandon all of us, like your father did your mother.'

This was Sunayana's last attempt to grab his attention and it worked. Janaka's instinct prompted him to react with rage, but with a massive effort, he managed to subdue his emotions. He attempted to answer her fears sympathetically.

'Someday, of course, I will have to leave. It is the Videha tradition. But, you have to remember that my father left only after fulfilling all of his duties. I am a king and I also have a family. I know I have to take care of our daughters and raise our son Bhanumat, as my successor.'

In the brief silence that followed, Sunayana wiped tears from her eyes.

'Then why do you not make Sita's marriage simple? Why do

you want to carry out the bow test? It is becoming an obstacle.'

'Sunayana! You know it very well. I have told you several times. This was what the sages had proclaimed,' Janaka replied flatly, his sympathy turning to frustration as he felt he was repeating himself endlessly.

'The sages! Forget the sages! You would find any excuse to keep her here. Why can you not come to a decision?' Sunayana said, visibly frustrated. 'Mithila is always threatened by war. If you marry off Sita to somebody soon, the problem will be resolved. We are in danger until then, and the sages are contributing to this!'

'She is not an ordinary person! An ordinary king or prince cannot marry her. What are you suggesting? Do you want me to have her wed in haste?' Janaka's eyes flashed with anger. 'I must do as the sages say, or risk attracting an evil eye.'

'She is already attracting an evil eye. It is you who is choosing to be blind,' Sunayana muttered acidly.

Silence followed, colder than the glass of milk that Janaka had left untouched by his bedside. He had been so certain that Sunayana loved Sita as much as he did. But now he was not so sure. She seemed desperate to get Sita out of the palace. Janaka had never thought of his wife as cold or heartless, but now, she seemed to be exhibiting signs of both.

'Every common woman is envious of the queen, but they do not know the plight of a queen. I want you to know that there is talk in the palace that you are not doing your duties. And I am so worried about this that I have lost my peace of mind. You left the only son we have in the hands of strangers. You separated him from me.'

Janaka did not reply. How much worse could this exchange get? Was Sunayana deliberately trying to hurt him? Ever since he had had that dream, everything that had happened in the palace had been unpleasant: a series of miseries, just like those he had experienced in the dream. And now its effects had seeped into the royal bedchamber.

※

Bhanumat, the youngest child of King Janaka, had been sent to Sage Vasishta's gurukul, the school in the middle of the forest, just a few years ago. This was yet another painful event that Janaka longed to forget. To reach Vasishta's gurukul, one had to travel many miles through the forest, over bridges made of twisted branches that hung low over dangerous streams. Wild animals of every species prowled the forest. But once travellers arrived safely, initiates could find a place where every art and human skill was taught. There, studying at the feet of experts and sages from many kingdoms, students could learn about everything: lessons on the afterlife, the Vedic sciences, the humanities, mathematics, physics and geography. Classes were held in engineering and architecture. The students spent days in the study of Ayurveda, of human physiognomy, cosmology, astronomy and astrology. They also learned military strategy. Daily, the young men practised the arts of self-defence, hand-to-hand combat, and attempted to master weaponry. They sweated and worked until they were exhausted, hardly eating and barely sleeping at night. But the education they received was not just theoretical. An attempt was made to apply it to the real life situations of the students, as they grew up and matured. The king hoped that when Bhanumat returned to the palace, he would be capable of ruling as a great king.

The family had been torn about sending Bhanumat to the forest school. But Janaka knew the importance of rigorous study.

He knew that if his young son stayed in the palace, he would become soft and spoilt by its pleasures, and become useless as a prince. Sunayana though, by this time, had developed a fear of anyone going to the forest. She did not want her son to take up the ascetic life, and certainly not in such a place.

Many nights, she would get up from her bed and walk to the courtyard to sit beneath the cold light of the moon, pondering these matters. In the end though, Janaka prevailed and her son was sent away, with a clean-shaven head, a loincloth, a jute bag, and nothing else. After Bhanumat left, Sunayana sat in the courtyard, weeping. This, she did many a night, and Janaka would comfort her, to assure her that it was best for the boy. He would be treated like everyone else at the gurukul. With no favours, he would live like a farmer's son, without maids, without servants, and he would become strong and immune to suffering.

Thinking of his son made Janaka wistful. How long had it been? But then a new terror made its way into the king's heart. If the malignant effects of his dream could make their way into the royal bedchamber, then how safe was his only son in the middle of the forest?

Whispers in the Night

Night at the palace was sometimes full of dread, especially when it rained. It was raining that night, and the rain beat on the earth as if to punish it. The lightning made grotesque shadows that danced like demons, heightening the dark mood of foreboding. Yet the people in the palace slept like the dead, as if to forget the terrors and disappointments of the last few days.

All the guards in the palace's female quarters were asleep except for the eunuchs, who kept vigil through the night.

Sunayana lay awake, listening to the sound of the rain. She had always been afraid of heavy rain, and whenever it poured like this, she would wake up. She felt that the rain was only a curtain of sound; behind it hid another mysterious sound, as if the whole world was crying. Sunayana knew that when it rained at night, one had to be awake, because anything could happen.

Her mind was tormented by a series of fearful images which prevented her from sleeping. Then, outside her room, even against the heavy sound of the rain, she thought she heard something.

She woke up her trusted maid, Malavika, and opened the door of the bedroom, peeping outside. She gasped. Silhouetted against a wall, in the dim light of a flickering oil lamp, was a human figure.

She shouted at the figure, trying to be heard over the

thunderous roar of the rain. The figure responded, striding towards her. It was Kushadwaja.

'Kushadwaja! Where have you been all this time? The king has been worried about you!'

'Has he?' Kushadwaja asked. He sounded sceptical. 'Is he actually worried?'

'Kushadwaja! Why are you talking like this? He is your brother!'

'He is more than a brother. He is a king. And sometimes I think, Sunayana, he is only a king,' Kushadwaja said, his chin held aloft.

'Tell me why you are here, in the women's quarters?' Her voice was husky.

'I will tell you everything, but before that, I need something to eat.'

The three—Sunayana, Kushadwaja and Malavika—stole down the darkened hallway in single file, past the kitchens and past the guards at the doors, their shadows dancing on the walls.

Sunayana and Kushadwaja sat cross-legged on a rug while Malavika spooned out bowls of lentils, fragrant with curry leaf, left over from the night's meal.

'Where have you been?' Sunayana asked calmly.

'The situation in the palace is unbearable. It is making me sick. I do not want to face my brother and I am trying to avoid meeting him,' Kushadwaja said, glancing furtively at Sunayana, as if trying to read her face.

'But if you avoid such meetings, do you think it will solve your problem?' she asked gently.

Kushadwaja replied, 'I do not know, but let me tell you. I told him repeatedly about the preparations related to the swayamvar. I warned him about Sudhanvan and his plan. He refused to take me seriously. Now all the blame is on me.'

'But it is not your fault that the guests did not come. I am afraid it is our destiny to suffer like this and our daughters will grow old without husbands. The more we delay their marriages, the more enemies we create. Now, almost all the kings of the world are our enemies, except, of course, Dasharatha of the Kosala kingdom. Why do you not speak of these matters to your brother?'

'Do you think that I have not? I have spoken to him many times, but these sages of his—who pose as advisers—are poisoning his mind. And worse than the sages is Mahosadha. I do not trust him at all. I think he is the reason for the woes of our kingdom. I have a strong suspicion that Mahosadha interfered in the letters of invitation to the kings for the swayamvar in some way. There is something wrong somewhere. If they had received the letters and confirmed to Mahosadha that they will come, why didn't they come?'

Kushadwaja continued, 'Unfortunately, the king does not listen to me if I say anything about Mahosadha. He is too much under his influence.'

Sunayana was about to tell Kushadwaja something, but stopped when Malavika entered with the food.

Malavika padded over silently, taking Kushadwaja's empty bowl and filling it with more lentil curry. She placed a few more rotis on his plate and poured a yoghurt drink into a silver cup studded with small rubies, and garnished it with a mint leaf. Kushadwaja picked up the bowl, and using the bread to mop up its contents, gobbled it all down as if he had not eaten for days. Sunayana, who had watched him grow from a boy to a man, smiled to herself. He was not eating like a prince, she thought.

She had always treated him with motherly affection. Kushadwaja had only been a boy when his father, Hrasvaroma, had left. It had caused his mother to lose all sense of purpose in her life. Severing all ties, even with her own son, she had fallen silent, resigned to a life of loneliness, haunting dark corners of the palace. Sunayana had then become Kushadwaja's mother and Janaka became not only his older brother, but his father as well.

Then Sunayana said, 'If I am to be honest, I have sympathy with what you say. Something deep within him seems amiss. He appears gloomy and melancholic, obsessed with this notion of the ascetic life. He has become...how shall I say it...unpredictable. I sense a deepening division in him between matters spiritual and matters temporal. I fear he may leave the palace one day, like your father did.'

Kushadwaja's face darkened.

'You are absolutely right. But, he says that my mind is poisoned. Let me tell you, it is not me, but my brother who has been blinded, especially by Mahosadha, who is positioning himself to take advantage of this situation. We should work together to try and help him.' He was trembling with anger.

'I agree. But what can we do? We are helpless here,' Sunayana replied.

'We can do something, but we must be in agreement that whatever we do should be right for the palace and the kingdom.'

Sunayana looked at Kushadwaja uncomprehendingly.

'In the epics and chronicles, there are many who play critical roles, yet their history is unwritten. There will be no chronicle of our efforts. But I believe it must be done,' Kushadwaja continued in a hushed tone.

'We are people with flesh and feelings, and we must live

in this world. For us, what is important is things happening around us. Not what is happening beyond us...My brother should know that he is a king.'

He continued. 'I know that it has been many days since he has looked at the tax revenues, but he has time enough to spend with his sages. Yes, it is true we need to have sages as advisers and to conduct the rituals in the palace. But there has to be a balance.'

'Is this true, about his disregard for the revenues of the kingdom?' asked Sunayana. 'I thought he had excluded you from such matters?'

'He is shutting me out of these affairs, but his peers have conveyed to me a message that, one way or another, is not my concern.'

'What do you mean?'

Kushadwaja's voice diminished to a whisper. 'Let me tell you one more thing. But please keep it to yourself. I trust you.'

'Yes. Go ahead. Of course.'

'I have come to know that I have been followed by spies who watch and report what I am doing.'

Sunayana was troubled. 'How do you know this?' She asked, also whispering now.

'I am sure of it, but what worries me is, whether it is by the king's instructions. Who do these spies report to?'

'No!' Sunayana exclaimed.

'Do not worry! I have laid out some plans. I will find out who is behind this. There are many such things happening within the palace, and I believe the king is not aware of them,' said Kushadwaja, looking around as if expecting to be overheard.

'You must have your suspicions?'

'I am unable to tell you right now.'

'You must speak to the king now, and speak to him boldly.'

'First, I want to make sure that what I have heard is the truth. And secondly, I need time with my brother—a private audience—but this, I am having trouble with. Mahosadha is always with him, like a shadow.'

Both sat in silence for a long time, sipping the yoghurt drink. Sunayana felt guilty, as though she was somehow being disloyal to her husband. Outside, the thunder resounded like the peril in her heart. An inexplicable dread pricked at her. Outside, the shower of rain stopped, and in the silence that followed, the sounds of dripping raindrops could be heard distinctly, amidst the shrill of the crickets. Nothing stirred, or so it seemed. But, outside a nearby window and unbeknown to both Sunayana and Kushadwaja, a furtive figure who had eavesdropped on their entire conversation was now making his way back to his master.

BOOK THREE
SANKALPA

*I am not other than Light.
The universe manifests
at my glance.*

2.8 ASHTAVAKRA GITA

The Prisoner

Janaka's father, Hrasvaroma, had set out to the forest when the young boy was only fifteen years old. Whenever Janaka recalled what had happened that night, his heart trembled. His mother's eyes had welled up with tears. It was his first experience of grief, and it had never left him. Hrasvaroma had gone to the forest, as his father and his grandfather before him had, leaving Janaka and his family in the palace, leaving all of his kingly burdens on his son's young shoulders. He had left the palace for a reason, to seek something beyond worldly needs and sensual pleasures, a tradition that had been followed by all the Videha kings before him. This call of the spiritual had come to each of the kings at some point in their lives; and when it did, they relinquished all that was wordly and left for the forest.

Janaka still remembered that night—the heavy rain beating the earth with its vengeful and unforgiving torrent. Hrasvaroma had set out from the palace and his mother had lost all courage, retreating to her chamber to weep.

Janaka had tried to follow his father into the night. But the king made the young prince halt at the lowest of the palace steps. It was there that he bade his son farewell. Beneath his thinning shock of white hair, his eyes had glinted mysteriously. He was a warrior going into battle with samsara, the world of constant rebirth, the labyrinth of temporal delusion. Janaka watched his father, half-naked, like a sadhu setting out to beg, grow smaller and smaller until the pitiless rain and the dark night had swallowed him up. But he was amazed, because, in his father's eyes, he had seen nothing but meaning and determination, not a speck of doubt nor an iota of indecision. That determination gave Janaka a tiny seed of courage to continue without his father. Everything that Janaka would need was conveyed in that last look between father and son. That final look had also given the young and inexperienced boy-king the courage to step into his father's shoes, as he dealt with the difficulties of kingship.

Ever since, whenever Janaka steered his horse into that great tangle of ancient trees, he could not forget the hurt he felt that fateful night and his heart would ache to see his father once more. When he was a young boy and in the grips of some childish fear, he used to lie down with his head close to his father's chest. Sometimes, he could still feel the heat from his father's hand, tousling his hair. Many a time, he had gone into the forest, sometimes on the false pretext of hunting, in the hope of catching a glimpse of his father, although he knew that his father would never appear. Besides, his father would never approve of this yearning as well.

Janaka was not the only one to suffer in his father's absence. In those felt first years, he often found his mother alone in her chambers, sobbing in the dark. Once, she held young Janaka close to her bosom, crying, and asked him, 'Why did he leave us? How could he leave us? Will you leave me too?'

At such times, he could not control his own tears. But he would somehow hide his feelings so that she would not see his pain. It was the last time she spoke to him. She spent the rest of her life in the dark corners of the palace, doting on Kushadwaja, never coming out of the prison she had made of her chamber. One day, she stopped crying and then, she never spoke a word until the day she died.

※

Janaka leaned on the turquoise balcony and surveyed the terraces leading away from the palace, their surfaces bright like rippling green silk. He could smell the fresh garden blooms; the aroma of the *thulasi* plant, and the sharp whiff of its distinct fragrance. As the warm golden rays of the sun caressed him, he was unexpectedly struck with a new idea. His heart pounded.

Janaka was ready for his ride. Below, Marut, his beloved black stallion, trotted towards the palace, clad in an intricately embroidered saddle, led slowly from the stables by an elderly servant. The horse waited impatiently for his master. He pawed the earth with his powerful hooves; he flicked his head a few times and then neighed with excitement. He had not been with his master for many days. Janaka dressed eagerly and descended a stairway from the balcony to the courtyard near the stables.

He mounted Marut, who shook his head, raised it high, neighed once again and then started cantering towards a path leading away from the palace and into the woods, as if he knew where Janaka wanted to go. Soon, he picked up speed, galloping through the palace courtyards, out past the orchard of pomegranates and then out from under a blazing sun into the cool shade of the forest.

Janaka liked to ride when his spirits were low. He rode when he felt lonely, he rode when his burdens were weighing him down, and he rode when he needed answers, into the forest, far from the palace and away from its schedules and problems.

He stopped for a while. A tiny butterfly descended on the

leaf of a hibiscus plant and the leaf bent and swayed under its weight. It flapped its wings and fluttered up and down. Then it flew away and disappeared into a nearby bush.

Janaka then paused by a brook. He looked down at the clear water and his attention was caught by the sight of a single, egg-shaped pebble. He slipped into the soul of the stone and for a moment, he was the cool and inviolable stone feeling the rush of the brook. Then he was distracted by the cawing of a bird sitting in the branches of a mango tree. He watched the bird, became the bird, flying to the next branch, floating in the air for a while, revelling the lightness of being.

For the first time since he was a child, he felt as if he was one with nature. He was not just observing. He felt like he was part of it, almost as if he was *experiencing* it. He could feel its vibrancy—not just out there, but within him.

Then, through the trees, he saw a peasant in the distance, ploughing the land with his bulls. The peasant was so engrossed in his work that Janaka imagined himself in his place. As he merged into the peasant's soul, he became one with him and felt the heaviness of the hard soil as he ploughed the earth.

As the boundaries of his ego dissolved, so did his cares. Janaka felt light in his heart. He had left behind him the burdens of many lives. A new existence was within him, an enchanting one. He felt that he had shed the excess marrow of his bones and discharged the poison stored in the bottomless depth of his being. He wanted to immerse himself only in the present.

Then, trotting down a narrow pathway, Marut and Janaka came to an open area with a little hut, like a hermitage, made of hay and palm leaves.

This was the hut where his father used to come to meditate. He had often accompanied his father here, when he was a child.

The tiny structure had only a small door at the front, so small that hardly anyone could enter. It looked like the hermitage was still frequented, probably by some ascetics living in the forest. The aroma of sap leaves mixed with wood smoke and ghee, and the remnants of a sacred fire were evidence of their presence.

On occasions, Janaka had practised meditation here with his father. Sometimes, the young Janaka would open his eyes and peek at his surroundings. Occasionally, a deer would shyly come out of the woods, and stand at the edge of the small clearing on which the hut stood, delicately nibbling tips of yellow grass.

Janaka tethered Marut to a nearby tree and sat down in front of the hut in the lotus position, feet crossed over thighs, his hands outstretched.

His eyes were half-closed, but his face was glowing. He felt the depth of the silence, like a vast ocean offering many untouched experiences. A cuckoo called and flew across the clearing. Marut snorted a few times and scraped the earth with his hooves. Occasionally, the sounds of animals and birds could be heard. Janaka struggled to stay inside the silence within.

Whenever he came here, he felt his father's presence. He always returned to the palace with a new energy, as if he were stepping into a fresh stage of life. New thoughts and new decisions would come easily to him then.

He got up and mounted Marut, but lingered on the horse's back for some time. A sweet breeze touched him. He felt he would miss this silence, this serenity. He gently nudged Marut's right flank. The horse came to attention and began to trot. All of a sudden, a fragment of his dream returned to his memory. In the dream, he had become a beggar. So had his father been, when he left the palace with nothing. Probably, he thought, this was his destiny, and this dream was a communication from the Supreme Being.

He then remembered what Sita had told him—that somebody would come to show him the way. The student is ready when his ego is tamed; then the master appears. Deep within him, he had felt that call. Perhaps his prospects would change now. He was excited, caught up in this delirium, quite unaware that Marut was riding towards the palace.

As he approached the palace, his trance was broken as he saw a long line of soldiers mounted on horseback, standing in a row. Mahosadha, mounted, was in front. Sunayana paced to and fro in front of the men, twisting the end of her sari pallu as she was wont to do when worried, her head bowed. Behind Sunayana and Mahosadha, Kushadwaja stood. All of them were silent. They all turned to look as he trotted into the courtyard. Janaka was shocked, as if he knew they had momentous news.

Sunayana's face was what held him. Her eyes took him back in time to somewhere in his childhood. Then all of a sudden, Janaka was struck with an insightful memory. Another wife, another woman, a husband who had gone away to the forest.

As soon as Janaka dismounted Marut, Mahosadha approached him. He spoke in a low tone.

'Oh, Maharaj! Everyone in the palace has been worrying about you since this morning. Especially now that Mithila is facing such a difficult situation.'

'Mahosadha! I am not just a king. I am also a man. Sometimes I need some solitude and peace.'

'Maharaj! I agree with you. But others do not see it that way.'

Janaka looked sharply at Mahosadha.

'Maharaj!' Said Mahosadha hastily, 'Of course, you have the right to peace and quiet. But you are also the king of Mithila.'

Janaka gestured to one of the guards to lead Marut away. He turned and faced the palace, its brilliant terraces, walkways and gilded turrets gleaming in the sun. He did not understand why all of them were ready and waiting for him to come back. Obviously, his reminders not to worry about his short disappearances had fallen on deaf ears.

But now he realized that a king has no freedom; in fact he has much less freedom than a common man. *A king*, he thought, *is bound by so many things that he cannot enjoy the charms of an ordinary life.* Neither could a king willingly choose the ascetic life. For a king, what is normal is the palace. What is normal are the courtiers, servants, ministers and the travails of constant threats and problems.

Janaka thought to himself: *How free a common man is! Free to think and to act! He can go wherever he wants to go, without hindrance.* Here, amidst his courtiers, guards and his army in his glittering palace, he, Janaka the king, was a prisoner. The glittering, gilded palace was his prison. It brought to him the image of a demon in the form of an enticing woman, in fetching clothing and glittering jewels, waiting to swallow its prey.

The Arrival

After many days and weeks, Ashtavakra reached Mithila. The long journey had tired him. His steps were slow and awkward. He had scratches on his arms and blisters on his feet. His skin was clinging to his bones more tightly than ever, and he wore hardly any clothes except for the coarse white loincloth girded against his hip. Even that was thick with dirt and ragged at the edges. He looked strange; his eyeballs had receded into their sockets, and they looked icy. Those deep-set eyes had something to say that was both intense and decisive, and they glanced to the sides only deliberately—like everything he did, with an obvious intention. He looked at the herd of a thousand cows near the palace gates, chewing and lowing, their horns beautifully adorned with gold and jewels. The king had offered them as gifts to anybody who could help him with his predicament.

Upon reaching the palace gate, he was stopped by a guard.

'Who are you?' Barked the guard. 'Why do you seek entrance to the king's palace?'

The guard was a gigantic man, his body covered in hair. He sported a large moustache that jutted out to sharp points, on either side of his face. He wore a huge turban and heavy bangles on his hairy wrists. He held a mace in his right hand, resting it against his right shoulder, and the sunlight gleamed off it, a silent threat.

Ashtavakra twisted his head in anguish at the guard's strange question and blinked. He had given little thought to his appearance, or the impression it would make on others.

'I am not a beggar, nor a thief.'

Ashtavakra was not pleased with the way the guard was looking at him. This was the kingdom of King Janaka, the well-known Rajarshi, the saint-king. Such a ruler should not stand for such shallow judgements. Ashtavakra remained still and silent.

'Who are you?' The guard repeated, in the same harsh tone. He kept his mace on his shoulder and stared into the sullen eyes of the stranger. 'Why have you come here?'

'I have come here to see King Janaka,' Ashtavakra replied.

'And what is the purpose of this visit?'

'I cannot tell you why. It is for the king to know.'

The guard was taken aback by the steadfastness of the boy.

'I cannot allow you to enter without the permission of the king. Anyway, what would a boy like you do in the king's presence?'

'I have come here with answers to his questions.'

The guard burst into laughter.

'There are already learned sages here in the palace, struggling to find answers to the king's problems. I suggest you go back to your ashram and come back when you are old enough.'

'Keep in mind,' Ashtavakra spoke quietly. 'That even a small spark can burn an entire forest. People do not simply become wise because of their greying hair. I am already learned in the knowledge I have acquired. But that is not for me to say. The king shall be the judge of that. Yes, a gate can be closed to those that bring ill, but it can also be opened to those who mean well. I cannot leave, so I shall stand to one side until you make your decision.'

Unnerved and lost for words, the guard looked at Ashtavakra once more, and then gestured to him to stand to the side. Ignoring him, he began questioning the visitors who had formed a line behind him.

Defeated, Ashtavakra had nothing to do except look around him. Many people approached the gate, and they were let in without question. Ashtavakra had a full view of the city. The shops were loaded with various articles such as jewellery, food items, brass and iron vessels and cloths. Customers scrambled from shop to shop, their arms full of purchases, while vendors enthusiastically hawked their wares. Each shop seemed richer and more lavish than the one before, as if they were competing with one another. The city and its inhabitants radiated an air of prosperity and carelessness, as garish and threatening as the glint of the sun on the guard's mace. Entertainment was aplenty: gypsies, jugglers, acrobats and many other people of that ilk. In the corners, drunks and ruffians quarrelled, raising their voices and hands over some silly matter or another. Everything here revolved around momentary joy, shallow displays of sensual pleasure, and beneath it all, Ashtavakra sensed the throb of an unending frustration and emptiness.

Wanting to shut himself off from this world, especially when people started to gather around him and point and giggle at his deformities, Ashtavakra closed his eyes.

But something about Ashtavakra's demeanour struck a chord in the guard. After the people had dispersed and Ashtavakra reopened his eyes, the guard met his gaze again. He saw a mysterious intensity in those glowing eyes. A lesser man would have become angry or upset at his questioning.

The guard dealt with such men every day, but Ashtavakra was obviously different.

'How can you remain so calm in the face of all these insults?' The guard asked Ashtavakra with genuine interest.

'Because, I am no different from you. Dignity is the guard at the door to my soul.'

The guard looked at him again. There was something about this boy that gave him pause. How many hours had he stood there waiting patiently, while people denigrated and abused him? He could tell that this boy was no ordinary person. And those eyes! It was the kind of eyes that often hid a secret world. Then he remembered stories, often told in guardhouses and taverns that enlightened men often appeared in disguise. Could this deformed boy be a Mahatma, a great soul? Gripped by the fear of being cursed by him, he bowed in front of Ashtavakra.

'Forgive me, Mahatma. I understand you are here to enlighten the king with your wisdom.'

The guard joined his palms and bowed to Ashtavakra once again. He opened the gate of the palace slightly, beckoning to Ashtavakra to step inside.

❋

Ashtavakra walked painstakingly past the other guards, every step a contortion of his twisted body. Though the guards at the gates and the people around him stared, the subtle look of warning in his eyes forced them to hold their tongues.

Walking thus unhindered, Ashtavakra made his way to the large assembly hall of the king of Mithila. He looked around in astonishment. His naked feet tingled as he walked on the polished marble. The giant statues carved out of rock, the soldiers in their gleaming armour, the furniture embellished with intricate designs, the carpet with its bold colours and patterns—all were new to his senses. But in his mind, he recognized their essence from the chronicles and scriptures.

The men were like demigods, adorned with earrings, necklaces and turbans. Extravagant silk robes hung from their shoulders. Ashtavakra was astonished to see such things, as he had heard about such luxuries only in epics. *This is unusual. How can a king be attached to such things and still be a saint?* He thought to himself.

Ashtavakra gazed at his surroundings with narrowed eyes and raised his eyebrows. He looked around for Janaka. What he saw around him was a gaudy, shallow, cheap imitation of real beauty; he found no satisfaction in the scene, only discomfort and disgust. Ashtavakra's solemn, serene face and demeanour, however, did not change.

Those assembled in the hall fell into a hush when they saw him swing into the hall with his distorted gait. But Ashtavakra boldly looked around at the courtiers, unabashed. Then, the entire assembly, including the king, burst into laughter. But to the surprise of all of the courtiers, Ashtavakra too started laughing, louder than all of them. He kept on laughing, until all the courtiers stopped. Ashtavakra was the last to stop. A deep silence set in.

'Respected king! I never expected that your court would be filled with shoemakers!' said Ashtavakra, breaking the uncomfortable silence. His voice, unlike his body, was strong and unwavering.

The courtiers exchanged glances at this arrogant remark. A wave of unease rippled across the court. What insult was this? How could a stranger stumble into the royal assembly hall and make such comments about the king's courtiers? For that matter, how did such a man get inside the palace? Whose permission did he have? They all waited to hear the king's response. Janaka stood up from his throne and announced, 'You have entered my palace without permission. And now, you are insulting my distinguished court. Who are you, to disregard these basic courtesies in my presence?'

'Respected king! You have already proclaimed your invitation across the kingdom, inviting learned men to engage in philosophical discourse with you, to help you with your predicament.'

The audience erupted in laughter, but Ashtavakra only smiled back at them.

'Here, I thought I was walking into a company of intelligent and civilized people. But I find that the people here are all of such little sense, that they make their judgements based solely on the physical appearance of a person. I could not help but laugh,' he said to the king. 'Do you not agree?'

Again, silence fell over the king's assembly.

'Why do you call them shoemakers?' Janaka asked curiously.

Ashtavakra smiled. 'Shoemakers in the market never look at your face; they only look at your shoes. They can judge everything about a person by looking at their shoes. They understand a person's wealth, his personality, whether he will pay or not...everything a shoemaker wants to know. A shoemaker can read a man's history and background by just looking at his shoes. A barber looks at your hair, a tailor looks at your clothes, and a shoemaker looks at your shoes.'

Ashtavakra continued, without hesitation. 'Although the river may be crooked, the water never is.'

'Those are wise words for one so young. Who are you?' Janaka asked. 'And what is the purpose of your visit here? Do you know that you are in the palace of Mithila?'

'Of course, I am aware that I am in the palace of Mithila. I have heard that you have offered many gifts in return for help with your dreams. Have you not?'

'Yes,' the king replied. 'Surely you have seen the one thousand cows outside the palace? They, and many more gifts, await the person who can enlighten me with the right knowledge. But, do you really think that you are the right person for this?'

'Respected king! Not only do I *think* I am the right person. I *know* so.'

Janaka was taken aback at the courage of the young man. But there came again the sound of laughter from around the assembly hall. The king raised his hands, signalling to his courtiers to stop.

'But, respected king! I want to ask you a few questions before we begin,' stated Ashtavakra.

'You may ask whatever you please.'

'I saw outside the palace one thousand cows, bedecked and displayed. And you said there are many more gifts waiting for the person who can help the king, with the right advice.'

'Yes.'

But are these gifts yours to give? Do these things—the wealth and the kingdom, actually belong to you?'

'Of course, they belong to me. I have inherited them from my ancestors.'

The courtiers were surprised at the king's patience in answering what they felt, were ridiculous questions.

'So who owned the kingdom before you?' Ashtavakra pressed on.

'My father.'

'And before that?'
'His father.'
'And after you?'
'My son.'

'That's very interesting. You are telling me that it was not yours before, and it will not be yours in the future. How do you become the owner of the kingdom, in between?'

The king suddenly realized that he had made a mistake. He was not the actual owner of the kingdom or its wealth; he was only a custodian. In a flash, he was awoken to the realization that nothing belongs to anyone. No one owns anything.

'All right,' the king said. 'I'll admit that these things do not belong to me. But I will give you what I actually own. I will give you my body.'

Ashtavakra smiled and said, 'O king, do you truly believe that you own your body?'

'Yes. Of course, I do,' Janaka could hear exasperation creeping into his voice. 'I have a body and I own it. And it is under my control. I can think and act the way I want.'

'Can you tell me where this body was a few hundred years ago, and where it will be a few hundred years from now?'

Again, the king realized his mistake. Even this body did not belong to him. It was given to him by nature for a span of time and it would go back to nature in the end.

The king did not know what to say next, and he looked at the courtiers. He sensed that there was some meaning in what the boy had said.

He was pensive. *Who is this boy? What is that fire in his eyes? Look at the way he carries himself and the knowledge he offers! Could this be the teacher that Sita had spoken of?* Janaka wanted to be sure.

'Then, all that I own, and that I can give you, is my mind.'

'Ha!' Upon hearing this, Ashtavakra burst into laughter again. 'How can you give something over which you have no control? Does your mind listen to you at all?'

All the people in the hall looked at the boy with a mixture of shock and bewilderment.

The king then realized that he was talking to a wise and righteous person. His face glowed and his eyes softened with respect. He bowed to Ashtavakra with his palms joined, and said, 'I am sorry. I realize my mistake. I really should think before offering anything to anyone. You are right. I do not know what is really mine.'

Jolted, the courtiers looked at the king. Murmurs began to reverberate. *What is the king doing? Has he lost his mind?*

Then Ashtavakra replied, 'O respected king! I am here to give you the answer you have been seeking. I am ready to enable you to receive the knowledge you desire.'

'Thank you,' Janaka said. 'For coming all this way. Welcome to my court. I have been waiting for you.'

Kushadwaja Asserts Himself

Senapati Mahadev hurried through the doors of the king's chamber. He found Janaka seated in the lotus position, on a low wooden seat, in the centre of the chamber. He was wearing a simple crimson robe. Sages, also in the lotus position, sat around him in half-circles, forming a crescent moon. Servants in loincloths sat nearby, fanning the king. Mahosadha, more resplendent than the sages and the king, in a silk robe and fine turban, sat on his right.

A sense of foreboding hung in the air.

'Maharaj!' Senapati Mahadev exclaimed. 'I must speak to you! However, it is a delicate matter.'

Worry stabbed at Janaka's heart, but outwardly he kept his composure. He glanced at Mahosadha and asked Mahadev to continue.

'Kushadwaja has been trying to interfere in matters of our defence and wants me to take steps in preparation against Sudhanvan. He has suggested that we sent troops out to intercept Sudhanvan, and perhaps engage in a skirmish to dissuade him from advancing further. But that would be a provocative act, with no merit. Mahosadha tells me to ignore Kushadwaja completely. But I do not know what to do in this situation.'

Janaka glanced at Mahosadha, then turned and spoke to Mahadev.

'Mahadev! Mahosadha is in charge of the defence of the

kingdom. There should be no dilemma. This is my final word on the matter.'

✳

Janaka and Kushadwaja strolled towards the far end of the palace. After having crossed the banyan grove and the orchard, they walked towards a little pond inside the woods around the palace. Lotus flowers bloomed in the pond where a tiny brook from the hills around, joined it. The pool of water was edged with piles of white stones. Janaka squatted at its banks and picked up one of the stones. He threw it into the water. The pebble touched the oval-shaped lotus leaves floating on the water and then descended into its depths with a dull splash.

'Tell me, what did you want to talk to me about in private?' Janaka probed.

'I have concerns about the way the affairs of the kingdom are being dealt,' Kushadwaja stated in a disappointed tone.

'I always thought you may have many things to talk about with me. But I know that I hardly ever have time to spend with you. Please speak freely,' Janaka replied.

'I know how busy you are,' Kushadwaja said gently and patiently. 'But Brother! We have to be very careful about who we allow into our palace. There is a danger that newcomers could be spies sent by Sudhanvan.'

'Why do you say that? Do you have doubts about any of our guests?'

'Yes. People in the palace are concerned about the stranger who arrived a couple of days ago.'

'Kushadwaja!' Janaka exclaimed, appalled. 'Ashtavakra is a young sage who has great wisdom! In fact, I have been waiting for him to arrive.'

'This is the problem. You are too obsessed with sages and ascetics, and now you welcome strange people into the palace. It is entirely possible that he is a spy, dressed in an ascetic's clothes and moreover, you have not even seen him before.'

Janaka blinked. He looked a little perplexed, unsure of how to handle Kushadwaja's statements.

'I was actually expecting somebody like him to come to the palace. For me, his visit is a manifestation,' Janaka replied gently.

'You know what happened in Kosala a few weeks ago. Ravana arrived in disguise and tried to kill the ailing Dasharatha. The king barely escaped with his life. As you are already aware of the threat from Ravana, how can you ensure that this strange boy is not him?'

Janaka raised his eyebrows and frowned.

Kushadwaja continued, 'If you take this stranger into your confidence, how can you be sure you will not discuss with him matters that pertain to the kingdom and its security?'

'Do not worry, Kushadwaja! He is not a stranger. He has come for a purpose.'

Kushadwaja's voice immediately rose, 'Are you blind to these dangers? Have my words no merit? I really do not think you understand what you are getting into.'

Kushadwaja gasped and his voice choked in dejection. He said, 'It is your decision. But I have something else to talk to you about.' He glanced at Janaka's face, but Janaka wasn't looking at him. His eyes were on the beautiful, pure lotus flowers.

'What is it?' Janaka knew that it would be another unpleasant statement from his brother.

'We still have not started acting on the threat we received from Sudhanvan. I think we have to act immediately, or else, we will all have to face the consequences.' Kushadwaja shook his head in anguish.

Janaka only nodded. 'I know. I am continually receiving information from my spies. I am well-informed—perhaps more than you think I am—and we are prepared for any such eventualities.'

Kushadwaja turned towards Janaka and spoke pedantically, 'You think you are well-informed. But you do not know what is going on behind your back. You have no access to the secret information that is circulating deep inside the palace. You do not hear any rumours, and rumours are nothing but the predecessors to untoward events.'

'What do you mean?' Janaka asked.

'You trust Mahosadha unconditionally, no matter what he says. You do not know what will happen eventually.'

'Please stop talking like this. Mahosadha has been our trusted associate for many years. We have won many wars because of his tactics and strategies. How do you think we won the battle against Kewatta?'

'That is what I want to talk to you about. You do not know what actually happened in the war against Kewatta. How did Kewatta know our secrets? Have you ever thought about how he knew?'

'What do you mean? You mean to say that Kewatta discovered our secrets from within the palace?'

'I do not want to tell you anything. It is better for you to check with Senapati Mahadev and the chieftains. You will find it out easily—if you are prepared to make the effort. If I tell you, you might think that I have something against Mahosadha.'

'How did you get all this information? I have never heard of such a thing. My dear brother, how can you be sure you have not been fed a bunch of lies?'

'Oh, Brother! I have completed my lessons in warfare. I have enough knowledge in the statecraft and tactics and strategies of the battlefield. I can organize and lead an attack on the enemy king and his armies. You should understand that after all these years of experiences, I cannot be taken for a fool.' Now Kushadwaja was furious.

'I am happy that you have learned all these skills. And one day your chance will come, my dear brother, but you have to be patient,' Janaka replied, pleadingly.

Kushadwaja stood still and when he spoke again, it was with resolve.

'Let me ask you something else. Why did Mahosadha plan to build secret ramparts during the war with Chulani? Everybody knew what was behind them. And can you tell me why Swapnapalaka, one of the chieftains, left so suddenly? He said that he is leaving for his village, but he never did. Later, we all came to know that he had joined Kewatta's group. And he was a close confidante of Mahosadha.'

Janaka listened without uttering a single word. His mind wandered and returned to the stones he had just thrown into the pool.

'Now, our situation is very different,' continued Kushadwaja. 'No one has arrived for the swayamvar. The insulted kings have joined together; they have combined their might and have created a united force against us. Mahosadha is your trusted prime minister. But we are all worried that if you tell Mahosadha everything, it might later turn into something else.'

We? Janaka thought to himself. *Who is this 'we'?*

Janaka walked a few paces away from his brother.

'And how long have I been telling you that I want to be

part of the effort to defend the kingdom? But you have never given me a chance. Because you do not have any trust in my abilities. To you, I am still a child! And you still keep thinking of what happened during the war against King Kewatta. That is in the past. Now, I have a solution for everything,' Kushadwaja spoke desperately, trying to get his clearly distracted brother to listen to what he had to say.

'A solution…? What solution?' Janaka asked.

'Let me organize the defence against our approaching enemies, Sudhanvan and his associates. Mahosadha has so many other responsibilities, like the revenues and internal affairs.'

Janaka darted a quick look at Kushadwaja and listened to him intently.

'I will be blunt…' Kushadwaja continued. 'We are all afraid that you have become obsessed with sages and the ascetic life. Most of the people in the palace believe that one day, you will suddenly go to the forest like our father did. And if I have to take control of the kingdom during such an eventuality, it is better that I have experience with some of these affairs. I believe defence is the best area to start with. I have just given you this seed of thought, and you need to think about it.'

With that, Kushadwaja turned and left. Janaka felt empty and alone. He sat by the pool for a while, waiting for the ripples in the pond to clear. When they did, he caught a reflection of his face on the surface of the water. He did not like what he saw. He looked old and worried, weary and burdened. Just then, he saw another reflection peering over his shoulder—the leering, cackling face of an old witch.

Turning around quickly to confront her, he was shocked to find that there was no one.

The Forest

The chariot drove into the forest, as far down the narrow pathway as it could go. When it ended, Janaka and Ashtavakra got out. The stunned driver was asked to go back to the palace immediately, leaving them behind.

Ashtavakra and Janaka walked further into the dense forest. It was dark, with tall trees such as oak, ashwood, banyan, peepal, neem and teak. Branches crackled beneath their feet as they walked. Sunshine beamed through the gaps in the large trees, subdued by the foliage and transformed into exquisite greenish tints, filling the wide-bladed grass with gentle light and shadow. A deer, startled by their approach, darted away in a rustle of dried leaves. The breeze brought with it the aroma of lemongrass, and Janaka felt connected with nature. He felt rejuvenated.

Janaka felt his father's presence somewhere in this very forest, and his heart both ached and swelled in joy at the memory. He had come at last to a place that was close to his heart, a long-forgotten home.

The forest path became narrower as they walked through the trees. Ashtavakra went first, with the great king of Mithila following him like an obedient student.

Then suddenly, Ashtavakra stopped as if he had forgotten something important. He looked at the king.

'What are you offering me as gurudakshina?'

For a moment, the king was taken aback. *Nobody is exempt from the desire of gifts and material wealth, not even this enlightened man.* But after a moment of contemplation, he quickly realized his mistake. In his thirst for knowledge, he had forgotten the importance of offering gurudakshina, the agreed reciprocity between a teacher and a student, a mark of respect, acknowledgment and gratitude.

But what could he give now? They were in the middle of the forest. He had brought nothing with him, certainly nothing that would equal the worth of the knowledge he would gain.

Should I remove my bright-coloured necklace, or my snake-shaped ring, or my silk robes adorned with beads, and offer those?

Ashtavakra stood, waiting to receive the gurudakshina.

'Ashtavakra, I do not know what I should give you. Can you tell me what it is that you want?'

Ashtavakra replied, 'I do not want any material things from you.'

Janaka blinked, unsure of how to respond. He waited for Ashtavakra to go on.

'All I want is your mind.'

'How can one give his mind, as it is within one's body? You have already taught me that one cannot give his mind,' Janaka replied.

Ashtavakra repeated, 'All I want is for you to surrender your mind. You cannot use it for anything else until I give you permission to do so.'

The king agreed to what Ashtavakra said, although he did not fully understand how such a thing could be done. Janaka sat on the ground on the narrow path, and closed his eyes. He worked to clear his mind in an attempt to follow Ashtavakra's command.

But even with his mind closed and his heart longing to focus, there were hundreds of thoughts—people, places and things—flashing through his mind in an instant. How could he surrender his mind when it was full of chaos? It had seemed such a simple promise to make, but it only took a few moments for Janaka to realize that it was the hardest thing in the world.

He opened his eyes and looked at Ashtavakra, who looked back at him and asked with a smile. 'What happened?'

'Ashtavakra, I am unable to control my mind. It is flying in different directions.'

'You have conquered many kingdoms, but are you finding it difficult to conquer your mind? True wisdom will appear only in a quiet mind.'

Ashtavakra paused a while, then continued, 'Is your mind still in the palace?'

'Yes, it is. Lots of things appear and disappear, and one thought leads to another and then, to another. The witch in the dream, the threat of war and a whole host of other things—hundreds of them flash through my mind in a second. I am thinking...that Sunayana does not like that I am away from the kingdom. Mahosadha is worried about my security. The sages do not condone what I am doing. And all of them think that since I am a king, I should be in the palace, focusing on the problems at hand.'

'Respected king, I understand. These are the voices in your mind. You do not know if they are real or not. But they definitely exist in your mind, because you keep worrying about them. Let me ask you something else. Even if there are problems like this, can you do anything about them now, when you are in the forest?'

'No. I cannot do anything about them now.'

'Then why do you want to keep worrying about them?'

'I do not know.'

'Can you solve such problems by worrying about them?'

'No.'

'Then why do you want to spoil the mind when you are aware that you can do nothing about them? When your mind is cluttered with thoughts like this, how can you enjoy the beauty you are surrounded with?'

'I know, but I cannot.'

'Respected king, your thoughts keep changing. There is an incessant flow of thoughts, appearing and disappearing. They are not the real you.'

'If they exist in my mind, how can they not be real?'

'The real "you" is different from those thoughts. You are reacting to every thought that visits your mind. By reacting to all of them, you are paying attention to your thoughts and feeding them, allowing them to exist. That is how a troubled mind creates a chaotic world.'

'So, what can I do now?'

'For now, the only way out is to pay attention and fully immerse yourself in what is around you. Live in the present, and understand that there is no moment other than the present. You are leaving the past behind and creating the future in this moment. Surrender to the present, and you can deliberately use the gateway of your five senses. Surrender yourself fully to what you experience. The real life is now.'

Janaka closed his eyes again and listened. He could hear the sound of the nearby brook, the chirping and twittering of birds, and the rustling of leaves as the branches above him swayed in the breeze. But he couldn't stay with it, as his mind began to stray in different directions.

Janaka opened his eyes and pleaded, 'I am trying, but I

cannot. Something is pulling me back, an unknown worry.'

Ashtavakra thought for a while and told the king, 'Can you drop everything and redirect your attention to your body?'

'How do I do that?'

'First, focus on your breath passing through the nostrils. Then be conscious of your inhaling and exhaling.'

Janaka tried to pull his mind away from his thoughts. He closed his eyes and inhaled slowly, savouring the sensation of air swelling in his lungs. A tingling rush of new energy flowed from somewhere deep within him, spreading throughout his body and rejuvenating his cells. The pulsing of his blood passing through his veins filled his consciousness, and calm washed over him as he became immersed in his body's sensations. The stillness centred him and he stayed like that for a moment. But the quiet within him didn't last, the remnant of an earlier conversation with Ashtavakra breaking his focus. His eyes flickered open and met Ashtavakra's steady, knowing gaze.

'That is the nature of our mind. It goes in thousands of directions,' Ashtavakra said. 'One is a fool if he believes he can control his mind.'

'Then what is the way out?' Janaka asked.

'Do not react to your thoughts. But be with them. Allow things to pass. Watch your thoughts. Be the witnessing self, and enjoy the game of the mind. It likes to bring all the chaos of the world. The mind needs to work on problems all the time and it will not allow you to stay in the present. The moment you realize that you are not in the present, is the beginning of your awareness. You are just touching the surface of consciousness.'

Janaka nodded, contemplating quietly what the man had said.

'The purpose of me bringing you here is to remove you from the highly distracting environment of the palace. The idea is to make you understand that there is something beyond the mind which is more important.'

Janaka listened in rapt attention.

'Do not fight to quiet the mind. Because when you fight, you are using the mind to fight. Just be. Whatever is happening to you, you have to experience it—sensations, feelings, thoughts—everything.' Ashtavakra paused, to see if Janaka was with him. Then he continued.

'Surrender yourself completely in the moment. What you see, touch, sense and feel now are the only realities in the world. Nothing else. Forget about the past. You are not in your palace. The enemy hasn't come to Mithila yet. Why do you want to think about things that haven't happened yet, and spoil the peace you have in you, when you know that the past and future are only some threads of your mind? Be in tune with your sensations right away.'

'How can I be in the moment, when the mind is darting hither and thither every instant?' Janaka asked.

'Just as you became aware of your surroundings a while ago, just as you were aware of your body a while ago, be aware of your thoughts. Every thought has form and you can look at them objectively. When you become aware of your thoughts, you can choose not to react to them. When you are not aware of your thoughts, you tend to react unconsciously to everything that passes through your mind.' He paused. 'When the thought of the witch passes through your mind, your mind is fuelling it, and you intensify your experience with more emotions, so you become scared and build it up inside your mind. You are unaware that you are a slave to your mind, unknowingly possessed by all that it tells you. And without you knowing, a sense of uneasiness has crept into your mind and attached itself to you. But if you are aware that thinking about the witch bothers you, you will realize that it is only a thought, created by your own mind. Take a moment. When you begin to watch your thoughts, you become detached from them. Then, you are no longer controlled by them, and you will find that the witch has no power over you.'

Janaka nodded.

'Then you will realize that you are not the thinker. The real "you" is behind the thinker. The real "you" is the witnessing self, an intuitive sense of experience, where there is no pain. There is only strength and happiness, joy and bliss. The beginning of freedom is the realization that you are not the possessed entity, the thinker, anymore. Only when you stop the chattering of the mind, do you create a space. And within that space, you will start realizing the deeper dimension of who you are. There, you will find the true beauty of life.'

※

When the chariot returned to the palace, Mahosadha rushed out to meet it. All the courtiers, sages and generals were assembled. With no king or Ashtavakra riding on it, a shocked and disappointed whisper washed over the crowd.

'He will return,' Mahosadha said, although he had no more proof of that happening than the others did. 'We must wait,' he advised.

Morning turned to midday. Without the king, lunch was a sombre and subdued affair. Mahosadha began to show signs of worry. It had been many hours now since Janaka and Ashtavakra had disappeared. The king had not only missed his lunch, but his regular medication as well.

Where did Ashtavakra come from? How can we be certain of his true intent? Doubts began to invade Mahosadha's mind.

'We must look for him,' he muttered under his breath, and a whisper began to spread through the chamber.

'My Lord?' One of the brigadiers approached Mahosadha, concern etched on his features. 'Please, allow me to go with you.'

'My Lord!'

Around him, the voices of the king's men rose in consensus. They would not be able to rest while their king was out in the forest with the strange, twisted little man.

'Very well,' Mahosadha announced. 'I will lead a small group into the forest. We must find the king and see him home safely.'

He strode out to the stables followed by the few he had commanded to go with him. The chariot driver was tending to his horses and turned to see the group arrive. He heard Mahosadha's concerns and agreed to show them the spot where he had last seen the king.

When at last they reached their destination, they found the king seated in the middle of the forest, not far from the point where the driver had left him that morning. He had his eyes closed, and he sat so still that he was almost immobile. Ashtavakra was nowhere to be seen. The officers were afraid that Ashtavakra might have cast some magic spell on Janaka to render him unconsciousness.

Mahosadha and his men stepped closer to the king, their feet coming down on the branches and twigs that carpeted the forest floor. The breeze quieted quickly, and murmurs of concern flew among the men. Janaka opened his eyes. He seemed to consider the situation for a moment, but in the end, all he did was to signal to Mahosadha not to come any closer.

'Maharaj,' Mahosadha said.

But King Janaka closed his eyes and did not open them again. He did not move at all. Mahosadha became frightened, and again, a murmur of discontent ran among the officials. The time of day when the king usually took his food and drink had passed and the king still had not stirred. Afternoon came, but the king did not move from his position.

Then Ashtavakra emerged from the nearby bushes, looked at the courtiers, and said, 'Why are you all so worried? The king is safe and everything is fine.'

He approached the king and spoke to him softly. 'Well, the ministers have come, the soldiers have come and many others have come. Why did you not reply to their entreaties?'

Opening his eyes, Janaka answered, 'Now, after experiencing the continuous no-thought state of mind, I realize that words and deeds are associated with the mind, and I offered my mind entirely to you. Therefore, before I can use my mind for anything, I need your permission. What authority do I have to speak to anyone or use this mind in any way, without your permission and command?'

'You are on the right path,' Ashtavakra said, 'Now we must begin our true work, with an empty mind. Ask your people to leave. I give you permission for that.'

Janaka beckoned Mahosadha and whispered a few words in his ear. At Mahosadha's command, the group of soldiers and courtiers retreated through the bushes, twigs snapping underneath their heavy tread.

Janaka turned to Ashtavakra and said, 'Ashtavakra, once again I surrender my mind to you. I now have a good sense of peace in my mind. It is very different from what I usually experience in the palace.'

'You will remain here in the forest for the rest of the day. You are not to use your mind for anything else. You must set out on this path with a clear mind. You are just now touching the surface of heightened awareness. This is your prayer, which is nothing but concentrated attention,' Ashtavakra spoke.

'Enlightenment means transcending your world of thoughts. In the enlightened state, your mind is only a tool that you know how to use when required. When you finished using the tool, put it aside. When your thoughts are not cluttered, you experience a smooth space deeper in you, where stillness and calmness set in. This is how you begin to experience a connection with your true nature. This is how you begin to awaken. This is where you realize that there is a bigger universe beyond you. In this space, you will fully realize that you are not the thinker. But you will take a step back and start watching the thinker. This is the first step to liberation, and the secret of all creation begins here.'

The Bow in the Hall

The Great Bow of Mithila lay in the middle of the palace hall, on a large golden table, bedecked in fine red cloth, with petals of fresh flowers strewn around it. Janaka joined his palms and bowed to the gleaming bow with his eyes closed, immersing himself in deep stillness. Occasionally, he chanted some mantras, silently. The fresh smell of flowers and the aroma of incense heightened the mood and the aura of the hall. His heart was filled with reverence. He felt drawn to the bow, as if his soul was being pulled into it. Janaka was a strong devotee of the bow, and he made sure that he spent time in prayers with it every day.

He opened his eyes and looked at the bow for some time. It had been in the palace for many generations, like a sleeping giant. The magic spell, which was subtle and dominant, flowed, and an invisible energy gently emanated from the weapon, infusing the air with its power.

He felt an enormous energy rippling through his body and his chest pounded with joy. An extraordinary courage with boundless power entered his heart. His senses seemed heightened. He could see every minute in a single glance, hear and distinguish all the many varieties of sound outside the palace—the chirping of the birds and the squirrels, the cawing of crows, the clanging of the swords from the soldiers' practice yard and the occasional shouts of men in the courtyard. He could hear everything, and he could derive a meaning from and connect with everything around him. He felt everything around him connected with a predetermined destiny—that this moment had purpose and meaning. A trance-like stillness crept into his mind, like a silent flowing river. He had never felt his mind to be so sharp and alert.

Janaka smiled; his face vibrant. How could anyone attack Mithila now? Who would have the courage to do so, and threaten its people? The reality ahead was like his mind—clear and smooth, without worry or fear.

I do not need anything. The bow and its energy are enough. If the bow will protect itself from being attacked or stolen, then why should I be afraid of anything?

Suddenly, he sensed something intruding into his domain, a disruption in his energy field. When he turned, he saw Kushadwaja and Sunayana waiting for him at the corner of the hall. They both took a step back, as if aware of their intrusion and how it must have seemed to the king.

Janaka realized they must have been in the hall for a long time, waiting for him to finish his prayers, awaiting a chance to speak with him. *What did they want to discuss? Is it something so severe that they have to look so solemn?* Janaka wondered.

A heavy silence hung between them and Janaka. They looked at each other. Who would begin? Whoever began the conversation would have the greater burden of responsibility for the situation. But one thing was sure. It was obvious that they wanted to talk about something very important and they were hesitating to speak. In the end, it was Janaka who spoke.

'It looks like you have something very important to convey,' he said calmly.

'Yes. Absolutely,' Kushadwaja said, visibly glad to be

relieved of the burden of breaking the silence. 'The people in the palace are worried about the looming war.' He hesitated a moment, and the silence stood between them like a stranger. Janaka signalled to him to continue.

'More than the impending war, they worry about your indifference towards it.'

Janaka waited for a while, smiled, and said, 'Am I expected to panic? Do you think that would help the situation? Why should I exhibit my worry? Like a fire, it can spread and lay waste to the land.'

'You know, this whole chaos revolves around two things: the bow and Sita,' Kushadwaja replied.

'I could not disagree more. They are not the problems here,' Janaka said, serenely.

Kushadwaja retorted, 'I believe time is proving that we need to look for alternatives to the swayamvar. How long can we wait like this? How long can we take this burden of the fear of being attacked? How many kings and princes have come here from faraway places to participate in the swayamvar, only to realize no man can win the contest?'

Janaka replied, 'We are kshatriyas—warriors. We are here for a grander, nobler mission. We need to protect the Videha dynasty from its enemies. We also need to preserve the legacy our forefathers have passed on to us.'

When Janaka said this to Kushadwaja, the latter shot a quick glance at Sunayana, who had a stony expression on her face. He stopped, looked at Kushadwaja, and continued, 'The long wait to find a suitor for Sita has meaning. It is part of a divine plan. We need to show patience. If the problems are trivial, we can try to solve them with simple and time-tested methods. But when they are bigger, these solutions will not work. Sometimes, it is intuition that is a vital tool. I have full faith that we are on the right path. This is my intuition.'

Both Sunayana and Kushadwaja were dumbfounded. They had never experienced such firmness from Janaka before. Kushadwaja was fumbling for words.

'But how can you trust the acumen of Satananda just like that?' he sputtered, finally. 'How do you know that his pronouncements on the bow test and the swayamvar were correct?'

'I am sure that the decision was right. What I knew before came as an answer through him. He was only a medium. What he said, only confirmed my thoughts. I felt it with my whole being. It was divine.'

'Do you not think it is risky? If it is not true, we could lose everything. The whole kingdom is under threat of an attack, because of this stupidly complex test. Many mighty men from all over the world have attempted it. None could even lift the bow. And the whole world says that it is a hoax. I do not think any human being can lift it. If we continue waiting for someone to come along and string the bow, we might as well be waiting forever.'

Sunayana interjected. 'Why do we not ask the sages to find another solution?'

Kushadwaja added. 'I would suggest the same; either we need an alternative, or we need to be prepared for war.'

'Kushadwaja! I cannot see any calamities befalling Mithila. Whatever is happening, it is happening for the best. This, I am sure is true, but like I said, I cannot prove it to you,' Janaka said.

Kushadwaja struggled for words. 'But the reality is that an army is on its way. So, what are you going to do?' Raising his voice, he continued. 'Are you going to bury your head in the sand and think that the stars will align themselves and we need do nothing?'

As he spoke, Kushadwaja watched Janaka closely to assess his reaction.

Janaka smiled at Kushadwaja.

'Do not worry, Kushadwaja. Everything will be for the best.'

'I really do not understand why you are so indifferent to the threat of an attack,' replied Kushadwaja, almost in tears. 'Our *lives* are at stake!'

Janaka stepped up to Kushadwaja and put his right hand on his shoulder, speaking sincerely and soothingly. 'My dear brother, let me tell you this. There is no war here. War is only the creation of a troubled mind. I have told you many times. If you become too obsessed about it, then you only encourage it.'

'What about the news we receive every day? And the undeniable reality approaching us?' Panic was evident in Kushadwaja's voice.

'What we want to know, we come to know,' said Janaka. 'What we want to recognize, we come to recognize.'

Kushadwaja looked at Sunayana, as if he did not understand what Janaka had just said.

'Do you not think, as the king, that you need to act more responsibly than this?' Kushadwaja raised his head and looked straight into his brother's eyes.

'Yes. Of course. I am doing that without wasting my time. Believe me. I can see that some people are unconsciously inviting the war here.' He paused for a moment, making sure Kushadwaja was listening. Janaka continued, 'Let me tell you something. No one will ever have the courage to come to Mithila anymore, not as an enemy. What makes it all the more disturbing is that these fears of war spread like an epidemic through Mithila, when it is our job to protect our people from this disease of the mind.'

There was no doubt in Janaka's voice.

Sunayana and Kushadwaja had nothing more to say. But they were not convinced. It was apparent on their faces.

Kushadwaja suddenly asked, 'Out of curiosity, can I ask—why are you spending so much time with Ashtavakra and the other sages when it is a time of emergency?'

'Oh, my brother! This time is no different from any other. We are doing what we are supposed to do. As I said only a moment ago, I am not wasting my time. I am using it wisely.'

Kushadwaja looked again at Sunayana, and hesitantly told Janaka, 'I believe you are looking at the problems philosophically. You are not dealing with the issues in a practical way. The result is that you are detached and you have become inactive. You are neither in the ascetic world nor in the king's world.'

Janaka was shocked by Kushadwaja's statement.

Kushadwaja continued, 'But let me tell you—there is something wrong in the palace. We thought it was our duty to inform you. We believe we did that just now. The rest is up to you.'

Kushadwaja paused for a while, but then spoke again, his voice trembling.

'Brother. I am trying to understand what you are telling me. However, my heart is also conveying something. The person you trust the most would bring trouble to the palace.'

Kushadwaja did not wait for an answer and left the hall. Having nothing more to say, Sunayana too followed.

Janaka stood alone, pondering over what he had just heard. They had come offering doubt and left him with doubt.

What should he do with these doubts? Should he doubt even Mahosadha, his most trusted adviser? But Mahosadha had also warned of deception in the palace. If these doubts grew, then surely there must be suspicion cast over all. Perhaps no one was an exception. If war was a disease of the mind, then surely doubt must be too? How many diseases could one mind have?

Kushadwaja's Escape

When Kushadwaja entered the large practice yard, General Mahadev was overseeing his troops in a siege drill. One group of men rushed against the other, simulating an unexpected attack. Swords clashed against each other with clanging sounds, sparks flying from the blades.

Upon Kushadwaja's entrance, Mahadev looked up. He left his men, crossed the yard to where Kushadwaja stood, and bowed to him as a sign of respect. The soldiers, following his lead, stopped practising and lowered their swords and lances. Their gazes followed Mahadev across the yard, but he gestured to them to continue their practice. Once more, the sound of clashing weapons filled the air.

'What can I do for you, Your Excellency?' Mahadev asked, respectfully.

Kushadwaja glanced at the soldiers, and then turned to Mahadev. 'How are the preparations going?' He asked.

'Preparations? I am not sure what you are referring to. This is a routine drill.' Mahadev furrowed his brow in confusion and glanced back at his men, as if to make sure they were not doing anything out of the ordinary.

'I believe...you are aware that Sudhanvan and his army are on their way to Mithila. They are already camping at the Sadarina river. It would be easy for them to reach Mithila, and we have to be ready.'

Mahadev looked at Kushadwaja, his eyes wide. This information was obviously new to him.

'Wh-what do you mean?' Mahadev asked, his face losing all colour.

'Why have you not begun to prepare for the attack?'

'But, Your Excellency! We have received no orders from Mahosadha or from the king.'

'I understand, and I respect the protocols. However, the kingdom is under threat of attack. And when the kingdom is under threat, it justifies any action. Protocol can and should be broken during times such as this.'

Mahadev frowned, and he looked worried. 'Pardon me, Your Excellency. We are unable to act upon such things without orders. That is the rule.'

'But you know that I am the king's brother and closer to him than even Mahosadha. I am telling you to do these things to protect Mithila and your men from a possible attack.'

'I understand, Your Highness. But I urge you to communicate directly with your brother, or to Mahosadha. On my part now, I will ensure we are prepared for any eventuality.'

❋

The next morning, Sunayana rushed into Janaka's chamber while he was getting ready to go to court for his regular sessions.

'What has happened?' Janaka looked at the gasping Sunayana, his brow furrowed in worry. 'Why are you out of breath?'

'Kushadwaja has left the palace,' Sunayana gasped. 'Did you have an argument with him yesterday?'

'No, I did not.'

Sunayana frowned. 'Then I am really concerned. Your brother

is worried that Sudhanvan and his forces are approaching. He is upset that you are not acting at all.'

Janaka seemed unfazed. 'My brother is loyal. He will return once his affair is complete. Why are you worried?'

'He has some close confidantes with him, and I doubt their intentions. They have gone to Sadarina to find out more about the situation. If he is found out, he will surely be killed by Sudhanvan. Why don't you send your forces to follow him swiftly and bring him back?'

'Sunayana! He has gone out on his own. He did not ask me before going. I am sure nobody in the palace knows about it—neither Mahosadha, nor the general who is in charge of the army. We cannot stop it.'

'But, you know that he sometimes makes immature decisions,' Sunayana pleaded.

Janaka bit his lips, restless, scanning the bright blue sky outside the window, as if it would provide him with an answer.

'Do you have any idea who went with him?' Janaka asked.

'No. I am worried,' Sunayana said. 'People in and outside the palace might blame you.'

'Why should they blame me for this? He has gone on his own.'

'They might say that you couldn't even command the loyalty of your own brother.'

'Sunayana!' Janaka shook his head with a smile. 'What he does is not in our control, nor is what others talk about. Why should we worry about what others say, when we have so many other issues to address?'

Sunayana's brow creased. 'They praise you in public, but I know that they criticize you behind closed doors. Of course, they have the right to do so. We cannot prevent people from talking.'

'What are you so worried about? Do you know anything about what he was doing?' Janaka turned towards Sunayana with curiosity.

'No, I do not.'

'If you know something, please tell me. We need to be prepared for the worst.'

'Do you not trust me? Do you not think that I would tell you if I knew something?'

'Of course,' Janaka thought for a while, still looking around.

'Is anybody out there?' he called to the guard standing outside the door.

'Yes, Your Highness,' the guard said, approaching Janaka.

'Summon Mahosadha immediately.'

✻

Meanwhile, high on a hill to the north of the palace a small group of horsemen watched as Kushadwaja and his confidantes came into view in the valley below. After pointing and talking amongst themselves, one of their number was dispatched north at great speed. The others pulled masks over their faces and charged down the hill. Their sudden appearance on the dirt path caught Kushadwaja and his men completely by surprise. Before they could prepare themselves against a possible attack, or even draw their swords, they were hemmed in.

Kushadwaja and his men, realizing that they were outnumbered, spurred their horses up the nearby hill, only to find when they were at its top that they were on a high cliff overlooking the Sadarina river. There was no way down, except into the raging cold river below that separated the kingdom and the Bhayanak Van. Nobody had ever survived its violent currents. Hopeless and outnumbered with their backs to the river, they dismounted and jumped into the waters, as the masked attackers approached. The masked men reined their horses at the cliff edge, and looked down at the tumultuous waters, creating ghostly silhouettes against the blood red horizon.

BOOK FOUR
MAYA

*Let the waves of the universe
rise and fall as they will.
You have nothing to gain or lose.
You are the ocean.*

15.11 ASHTAVAKRA GITA

Wild Rumours

It was the time allocated for the king's spies to report back to him. Today, Janaka wanted to hear directly from the spies, without having their testimonies filtered by anybody else.

He had only a few such confidantes who could be trusted with the responsibility of gathering intelligence and providing feedback. Baleshwar was one such person, a shrewd man who was also known for his prudence.

'Now, Baleshwar, what do you have to report?'

'Oh, Your Excellency! What I have to say may not be to your liking,' said Baleshwar, clearly distressed.

'Of course. You know me. You do not need to apologize, or give any sort of introduction. You may go ahead.'

'There is a rumour in north Mithila that Kushadwaja has abandoned you and left the palace because you have not responded to the threat of war. They say that you were advised to prepare for a siege, and that you ignored their advice, and that your own brother has abandoned you because of it.'

'Are people so afraid of war, even that far in the north?' The king's gaze grew distant, and his features crumpled in sadness.

'Yes, my Lord. The people still remember the tough times, the challenges that all of Mithila, including the north, once faced. These days, they have been quite comfortable, but those memories are fresh enough that they live in fear of any minor threat of war or natural disaster...'

Janaka nodded. He heard the words that Baleshwar uttered, but his heart fell into a deep darkness. It troubled him deeply that his people felt this way. How could he alleviate their fears?

Baleshwar then left the palace, but in accordance with his craft, sought the anonymity, cover and bustle of the market before making his way back north. He dallied amongst the hawkers, jugglers and acrobats feigning interest, occasionally smiling and buying the odd cheap trinket. Then he stopped before an old snake charmer and watched as he finished his act. Baleshwar then politely applauded and handed the snake charmer two coins. Between the coins was pressed a neatly folded, freshly written note.

※

Sunayana was not the only one who was growing concerned. With or without the king's permission, consciously or unconsciously, the people in the palace were preparing for war.

The cooks grew stingier and stingier with their portions, accumulating food in the stores beyond the kitchen and using as little water from the reserves as possible. The soldiers trained longer and harder than was required of them, staying late in the grounds, keeping fit and in practice—the stress of an impending war pressing upon them. The people themselves grew quiet and nervous, and even their celebrations seemed muted.

Sunayana missed none of this, and the king's courtiers seemed to have noticed that she, unlike her husband, was fully aware of and attuned to what was happening around. Many people in the palace began to come to her with their questions about Kushadwaja and his departure from the palace.

Why, instead of acting to protect the palace against imminent danger, did the king choose to organize consultations with his sages? Why, with a real threat looming over his kingdom, did he see fit to indulge in a sort of spiritual game? Why would a responsible king ignore such news and seek only to escape to a different world?

Sunayana did her best to address her people's concerns, but she could see that they had already begun to draw their own conclusions. The sages, surely, had appealed to the king, seeking only to increase their own wealth. Perhaps they had taken advantage of a frivolous mind caught up in the fallacy of spiritual search. This, surely, was not their ideal role. Were they not supposed to advise the king at the right time?

And what about Mahosadha? He was a sensible person who should understand the threat to the kingdom. Sunayana thought. *What if Kushadwaja told the truth about him? Why doesn't Mahosadha influence the king, when he is aware of such a need?*

The people were confused. What is more important for a king than protecting the lives of his subjects? How could he spend his time seeking knowledge for his individual fulfilment when he had the bigger responsibility of the kingdom and its people to concern him?

Again and again, the residents of the palace brought their concerns to their queen, and one by one, Sunayana did her best to calm them.

And yet, the rumours continued to spread. Sunayana could only watch as the faces of the people around her grew graver and more lined with concern. She could do nothing except her wifely duty, which was to support her husband, and her duty as queen, which was to support and uphold her people. But Sunayana was beginning to wonder if there was anything she could really do for Janaka or for Mithila.

The king was afraid to lose Sita, the people said.

Sunayana did not really think, or did not want to think, if that was true. It was true that her husband loved Sita, as did Sunayana and her younger daughter and nieces. But she could not imagine he was capable of such selfishness. It simply did not match the concern she saw in his eyes daily. He truly wished to see Sita happily married and the kingdom at peace. Sunayana had no choice but to believe these things.

And yet, she was also growing anxious. Sunayana loved Sita as though she was her own child, but she had her younger daughter Urmila and her nieces, Mandavi and Srutakirti, as well, to think of. It would be improper for them to become engaged before their older sister was married. The queen found herself increasingly anxious for Sita's suitor to appear, and with his divine skills, fire the arrow from the bow.

This matter with Kushadwaja also weighed heavily on her mind, and there was no one to whom she could turn to. No one, not even Mahosadha, nor his army chief, nor his ministers, nor his advisers, had been able to discern what had truly happened to Kushadwaja.

The king had once told her, 'Kushadwaja went somewhere on his own, and there is nothing we can do but wait for him to come back. We should not interfere in his decision. My brother is not as foolish as you think he is. He will understand the truth and bring the truth home with him.'

But still her mind raced. It was all becoming too much, thought Sunayana to herself. She needed to try to stop worrying, even stop thinking. Routine might help, as it often did, so she dismissed her servants, prepared to retire, and ordered some food. Staring out of the window, her responsibilities as mother, wife and queen weighed upon her. She wondered if she would find peace, true peace, ever again. The night was warm and its music quietly vibrant, but all Sunayana could hear were the incessant sounds of her own dark thoughts.

Then, almost to her relief, she heard a voice at the door. *It must be the food.* Distractedly, Sunayana opened the door. To her horror she saw not a servant bearing a plate of wholesome food, but instead the carcass of a crow lying on the ground, staring malevolently at her.

Seeking Liberation

Days passed, with Ashtavakra and Janaka debating, the sage discoursing and the king, questioning. Often, they secluded themselves in the king's chambers, with instructions that they were not to be disturbed.

That day, Janaka started with Pranayama, the breathing practice where breath is intentionally altered to a certain rhythm. Each time he inhaled, he was aware of air passing through his nostrils and into his lungs, bringing new life to him. The length of each breath grew deeper until he became the breath passing through him. All sense of physical body disappeared. Sensations took over thought. His presence extended beyond his mortal shell, and he was everywhere. He was calm, like a flowing river; like a feather, he floated in the air.

Janaka opened his eyes slowly. He sat unadorned, shorn of the trappings of kinship. His lips were curved into a smile. Ashtavakra was ready, sitting in the lotus position in front of him on a mat of bast fibre, wearing only his loincloth. Beside him was his jute bag, in which he carried books made out of palm leaves covered by thin wooden boards on either side and bound with stained threads. He was relaxed, and when his eyes shone, a childish curiosity throbbed in them.

After a pause, Janaka told Ashtavakra, 'I want to attain what you have attained. Can you teach me how to get there?'

Ashtavakra's face glowed at Janaka's question.

His answer, however, was unsatisfactory. 'Respected king!

What is it that I have and you do not?' The question was an impossible one, and yet the expression on the sage's face was calm, more soothing than reproachful. 'You already have everything that I do. There is nothing more I can give you.'

Janaka could not tear his eyes from Ashtavakra's soothing countenance. He continued. 'Looking at your face, I can understand that you are a liberated being. But I do not understand how you have attained such perennial calmness and liberation at such a young age. How can I attain liberation in the flash of second? Please teach me how to reach atmajnan or self-realization.'

Ashtavakra's face remained expressionless. Janaka spoke excitedly. 'I know that it is possible to shift myself from the restrictions of time to eternity. I see from your example that it is possible for a man to transfer his relative conscious to the absolute, and therefore, travel from bondage to liberation.'

Janaka paused for a while and then continued, 'Ashtavakra, I have seen that you do not practice. No rituals, no observations. Yet, I can see the glow of perennial peace and calmness in you. In the palace, we do a lot of rituals and engage in a lot of practices. But now, I believe it should be possible to do as you have done, to achieve such a state with no rituals, no chanting and no control over breath or thoughts. Now that I feel I have touched the surface of bliss, I know that I am close to eternal bliss. How can I transcend my body and become a true Videha, a bodiless king?'

Janaka stopped speaking, but his body trembled. His eyes were wide, and his mouth was turned up in a child-like smile. Curiosity had made him young again, and he hungered for Ashtavakra's guidance.

Ashtavakra looked closely at the king, examining his expression, and he nodded slowly. 'Yes, I understand what you desire.' He leaned his crooked body forward, sighing with empathy as he continued to gaze at the king.

'Your desire is again, a craving of the mind. Just be. Realize that you are already there. You do not need to break the door when you have the key with you.'

The answer was not enough for Janaka. 'So how do I do that?' he pressed.

He smiled and waited for Ashtavakra to answer his question. But Ashtavakra only said, 'Such a state cannot be attained through intellectual exercise, or by any sort of practice. It can only be understood by your heart, by an intuitive spiritual experience.'

Janaka nodded. 'But how do I do that? How can I attain that in a moment, in an instant? By mounting a horse? Upon opening my eyelids?'

Ashtavakra listened, taking in the king's request and said, 'Tell me, respected king, what do you want to achieve?'

'I know that I can push myself into a state where I can transcend the temporal world. If I were to achieve that, I would not feel any of the miseries of the world. I would be free from my mind-made clutter. How can I be illuminated by that instant bliss and become truly happy? I seek the 'light' that illuminates me and everybody around me. What is that light, and how can I get it? How can I ignite that spark inside of myself?'

Ashtavakra said, 'Just be.'

Janaka looked at him bewildered.

Ashtavakra continued, 'Just be the witnessing consciousness.'

Janaka still didn't seem to understand. He looked at Ashtavakra as if seeking further explanation.

Ashtavakra replied, 'Imagine you are in a dark room. There are so many things in the room, but in the heart of the darkness, you do not see them. Now, imagine you have a torch with you. The moment the light from the torch appears, things in the room become visible to you.'

Janaka listened intently. 'That is consciousness,' Ashtavakra continued. 'Because you are the torch, you are the light. These things appear and exist for you, only when you become the witnessing consciousness. Your ability to separate yourself from, and see yourself as the witnessing consciousness, gives you the energy to examine who you are and transform to what you want to become. It allows you to see what you want to see and do what you want to do.'

Janaka nodded, imagining the room and the darkness, feeling as though he had experienced it all.

Ashtavakra continued, 'And being the witnessing consciousness, you have the ability to either see those things as real, or to shut out the light and accept that nothing exists in the darkness around you. Then, even to the darkness that surrounds you, you can give light. Whatever you see around you is nothing, until and unless you give life to it. Your worries, fears, apprehensions, doubt—everything exists because you give life to it. You give life to them, for them to exist in your world.'

'You mean, I create everything around me?'

Ashtavakra cracked a crooked smile. 'Now you understand. You give life to the world around you. You create everything, even yourself.'

During the time Ashtavakra was in the palace, Mahosadha had barely been able to speak to the king. Janaka had been holed up for days in his chamber, with eyes and ears only for the young sage. Every time Mahosadha thought he would catch Janaka for a quick word, the king would speak of some other story or insight that excited him, and would seclude himself once more.

On this particular day, the duo had been in the chamber since morning. Mahosadha and Senapati Mahadev had been waiting outside the door for hours with an important message. The king had not emerged once—not for the treasury, not for the military, not even for the public audiences that he had once considered so important. Nor had he spent time with his family or indulged in any of the religious activities that he so loved. The task of dispatching letters and receiving information from the spies had fallen to Mahosadha, who felt as if he was being pulled in a dozen directions all at once, trying to keep up with his own responsibilities as well as the king's.

Dusk was approaching, and Senapati Mahadev was pacing back and forth in front of the chamber door. He found himself glancing repeatedly over his shoulder, as though the invaders would come upon him right there, at that moment, in the corridor. He felt a quiver inside his stomach, and a chill passed through his body. He couldn't stand still, but as he walked back and forth, tracing circles in the hallway, he couldn't help but feel that he was mirroring the kingdom's current path.

From within the chamber, they could hear the occasional bursts of laughter. From outside, the drums sounded as the regular shift of guards changed, as day changed into night.

Mahosadha's patience was wearing thin. He said to Mahadev, 'O Senapati! It looks like the king is caught up in a delirium, and the little twisted sage has cast some spell on him. I think it is important to warn the king and slowly pull him away from the clutches of this strange boy.'

Mahadev looked at Mahosadha in astonishment.

Mahosadha continued, 'I think I can do this on my own. I may need some privacy with the king. I will call you when the time comes.'

Senapati Mahadev nodded and left.

The World We Create

'You give life to the world around you. You create everything, even yourself.'

These words from Ashtavakra resonated within Janaka. He asked curiously, 'What do you mean?'

'It is you who creates your very existence in the moment of your choices.'

'So, how then do I attain moksha, or liberation?' Janaka asked.

'You are already liberated,' Ashtavakra replied. 'Why do you want to be liberated again?'

Janaka was puzzled. He looked into Ashtavakra's eyes, but when he did not find the answers he was looking for there, he asked again, 'What do you mean?'

'You are already liberated. It is only that you do not realize it.'

'I do not understand. Can you explain further?' Janaka's face creased into a deep frown. He rubbed his chin, trying to understand what Ashtavakra was telling him.

'Your existence has already given you everything. It has given you a wonderful life and beautiful eyes with which you can see the beautiful world—the garden, the flowers, the rivers, everything. You can hear music from the birds. Nature has given you everything. Why, then, are you asking again like a beggar for more than what you have? Know yourself that you are already liberated, and know yourself as the witness.'

Janaka heard Ashtavakra's words and understood what they meant, but deep within he was still searching for answers.

Ashtavakra, picking up on his confusion, went on. 'You don't probably realize it because you are limited by the physicality you carry. But the truth is you are a non-phyiscal being. Simply be an observer. Your body is made of earth, air, fire, water and ether. But you yourself are none of these elements. The real "you" transcends your physical identity. You don't know this truth, because your perceptions are limited with your five senses and the time-space reality. Just realize that you are the consciousness. You are the torch with which these are illuminated. You are neither a king nor a sage. You are unattached and formless, nothing but the witnessing consciousness. Just know this and be happy.'

Janaka became silent and contemplative.

'You are liberated now,' Ashtavakra urged. 'You have already attained moksha, if only you could realize it. There is no past and no future. Whatever happens right now is the truth. Life is now. Liberation is now. Freedom is your nature, and the whole of your existence is made of freedom. And you can access the world of freedom now. Be liberated right where you are, because you are already awakened and enlightened.'

But Janaka still could not grasp fully what the sage was saying, and looked enquiringly at him, hoping for more explanations.

Ashtavakra continued. 'To make it easier for you, let me tell you a story.'

'Once there was a king who was so angry with his son that he sent him into exile. The son wandered far until he found himself on the streets of an unknown village. He did not know any trade or profession because he was the son of a king. As he did not have a trade, he started begging. Without his palace, there was nothing else that a prince could do. But he could not tell people that he was once a prince, because nobody would believe him. So, begging was his only choice.

First, he joined a group of beggars. He lived with them, slept with them and ate with them. He waited in the queue at weddings for leftovers, waited outside homes for hours hoping to pick up some scraps and sometimes fought with animals for food. Several times, he told his peers that he had once been a prince, upon which all of them would laugh and mock him. He tried to convince them many times, but he was never taken seriously. So, he stopped talking about it and pushed the memory of his time as a prince to the back of his mind. He forced himself to forget this memory, setting aside his identity as a prince. The prince went on begging, and twenty years passed by. With time, he almost forgot that he had once been a prince.'

Janaka listened to the story with almost child-like curiosity. He imagined himself in the place of the prince. He experienced the anguish and feelings of the prince. In doing this, he was trying to understand what Ashtavakra was attempting to reveal to him.

The young sage added, 'Can you see? This is how we even forgot who we are and where we come from.' He then continued the story.

'His father, the king, became old and sick. He spent all of his days in bed. He was worried about his kingdom and began to wonder who would rule it after he died. Since he had only one son, he called his ministers to his bedside and ordered them to find his son, wherever he was. The king then told his ministers to inform his son that he had pardoned him.

The ministers searched for the prince throughout the

kingdom, and after many days, they found him, naked and begging with a broken bowl in front of a house in a distant village. His face and head were unshaven, his hair long and unkempt, his eyes dark and sunken.

The chariot stopped near the beggar prince, and one of the ministers, recognizing the future king, fell at the feet of the beggar. The beggar was taken aback to see what was happening in front of him, but in a flash of a second, he recalled that once he had been a prince. For twenty years, he had forgotten his real identity. But in that moment, the memories of that life came back, fresh and vivid. He tossed his broken begging bowl away and ordered the ministers to organize a bath and find him some fine new clothes. His entire transformation from a beggar to a prince occurred in the blink of an eye.

He was still the same person, but once he transformed back to a prince, his father's ministers and the train of servants with them bowed to him, respect welling up in their eyes. The prince's face became radiant, and he jumped with newfound energy, mounting the chariot. In that instant, his forehead grew broader, his face took on a glorious vibrance and a bountiful joy shone in his brilliant, youthful eyes.'

There was a pause.

Then Ashtavkra said, 'You have traversed this long journey for decades, without really knowing who you are. You were never aware of your true nature, much like the prince in exile in my story. You have struggled, wandered and begged…'

Ashtavakra paused again.

'Now wake up. You are not a beggar anymore. You are the ruler of a kingdom. You are the ever-powerful and omnipotent. You are liberated.'

Janaka's eyes shone now, blinking, as his perceived world

and the new world merged, making him understand what Ashtavakra had been saying all along. The story had awakened an insight, one that made him look past the veil of physicality. The moment the realization happened, he felt his energy connecting to the world around him. The vibrations shot through him, making him elated and exhuberant. His heart throbbed with the new spirit that sprouted from within him. He wanted to embrace Ashtavakra, his guards, the palace itself and the world around him. He felt more in tune with his surroundings than he had ever been.

The connectedness he felt extended to every object in his room, big or small. The energy from him and everything around him, merged in a flow. He had awakened.

Ashtavakra smiled and said, 'This is your true state. Anything else you see around you is but an illusion of your mind. You give life to these illusions with your conscious energy, as if giving light from your torch. And you have the power to cause them to cease to exist, as when you extinguish your torch, or cast its light elsewhere. The moment you realize that, you are transported to a different state. It's not a matter of thinking these words with your mind; it's a matter of feeling their truth with your heart.'

Janaka felt something significant had happened in him. Now, when Ashtavakra spoke, there was no confusion, no doubt. There was only the sense that he was being told something that, somehow, he had already known.

'You are not your body,' Ashtavakra went on. 'And you are not your mind. You are nothing more nor less than your awareness, the ever-witnessing consciousness. You are neither a king nor a husband. Neither a father nor a brother. You are nothing but pure consciousness. If you think you are bound, you are bound. But if you think you are free, you are free.

Simply thinking, and believing, makes it so.'

Janaka nodded.

'Over the years, you have been conditioned to think you are your body and mind, but you need only a split second to come out of that, and to see the truth. Just as it took the beggar only a moment to realize he had been a prince all along, the moment you realize this, you are liberated. No. You are already liberated. I am not telling you anything that you do not already know. There is nothing new coming from me. Just as the waves come from the water, this realization is coming from within you.'

✷

When at last Janaka came out of his chambers, he looked very different from the king that Mahosadha knew. In the midst of his worries about his dreams and Sita, the king had, of late, seemed to be ageing rapidly. But now his face was beaming with a youthful radiance, and his eyes, which had been so clouded by troubles in the recent past, were wide and glowing. There was a bounce to his gait, and he approached Mahosadha with his mouth half-open, as though about to share some joyous news.

Something about the expression on Mahosadha's face stopped him, however, and instead, he asked, 'What is the matter, Mahosadha? How long have you been waiting for me here?'

'My Lord!' Mahosadha exclaimed. It was as though the news he had been holding in his chest all day was desperate to break out. 'I have something urgent to discuss with you.'

Janaka nodded, and while the light in his wide eyes did not fade, the line of his mouth grew grim.

'It is with great difficulty that I bring this news to you,' Mahosadha said, and his voice trembled. 'I...am not quite sure where to begin.'

'Mahosadha, go ahead. You can tell me directly,' Janaka said calmly.

'The spies from Sankasya have brought us some troubling news. There is somebody within our palace who is part of Sudhanvan's plan.' Mahosadha's expression was pained. He watched the king's face, half expecting it to reflect anger and despair.

'Who is that person?' Janaka's features twisted, and his brows knitted together.

'Maharaj! We wish it wasn't necessary to tell you his name. I am afraid that it will devastate you to learn who the conspirator is. But the situation is grave. Please understand we have no other choice here.'

'Why are you avoiding the question? Please go ahead,' Janaka replied.

'I've thought about it many times.' Mahosadha wrung his hands together; they were trembling and cold with sweat. 'I've debated whether or not to tell you. I have heard from the spies that he had a deal with Sudhanvan. He would help Sudhanvan defeat you, and in exchange, he would get the kingdom of Mithila, while Sudhanvan would get the bow and Sita's hand in marriage.'

Janaka's expression did not change, but a note of impatience crept into his voice. 'And who is that?' he asked.

'Your brother, Kushadwaja, my Lord!' Mahosadha let the words out in a pained sigh.

Janaka turned pale, reading the apprehension in Mahosadha's strained face. He took a step backward, all emotion drained from his visage. He considered his next words for a long while, attempting to reconcile what he knew of his brother with this news that Mahosadha had just brought to him.

The Rope and the Snake

Fear started settling in the palace like an uninvited guest. The sense of foreboding spread everywhere. The residents of the palace went about their every day lives, as if it was their last day on Earth. Deep, profound silences prevailed, even as rumours spread, travelling through the dark corners like evil portents. Women and children woke in the middle of the night troubled by wild, violent dreams. The king's commander-in-chief and his soldiers were on the edge. The king had not approved any preparations for war. But deep within the closed quarters of the palace, everybody was talking about the threat of war.

But the signs of doom were everywhere. Outside the palace, crows cawed raucously. Anxious, bucking horses became almost impossible to ride. The wild roars of elephants and the thumping of their feet shook the ground. Even the trees outside the palace seemed to stand still, as if afraid of what was to come.

However, to everybody's surprise, King Janaka and Ashtavakra continued to spend time immersed in their discussions in the midst of all this chaos. They existed in a world within, where the oppressive gloom that had settled over the rest of the palace could not touch them.

'O Ashtavakra! It appears to me that two worlds exist now. There is a world full of fear, with threats, on one side. But here, we are in a different world. Although I know that nothing will happen, I have this doubt—which one is right? Is it the world that all of Mithila has accepted, or the one I fully believe in?'

'Definitely, the world that you believe in is your world. That's the difference between you and others. That's the only way you become a true Videha.'

'But, you see, the worlds are very different. One is a world of fear and threats, whereas the other is a world of peace and love. How can both the worlds exist in one place?'

'O King. They are not different, and if you know the truth, you would know that both worlds come from one source.'

'What do you mean?'

'O King! Have you forgotten your dream? In the dream, you were a beggar. When you woke up, you were king. If these two realities can occupy one mind, why can't it happen to a kingdom?'

Ashtavakra continued. 'In the dream, Mithila was attacked by neighbouring enemies. You were hungry and you had to beg for food. All the people you approached shut their doors on your face.' Janaka nodded.

'But when you opened your eyes, the village had vanished and the court appeared. You realized that you were not a beggar—it was a creation of your mind. The events that happened in the village were made from your indivisible mind. There are multiple and diverse objects and events around us— all of them come from you—the source. They are like two pots made from one kind of clay. We have been made to believe that all things are distinct from one other. But the truth is that everything comes from one source, a single indivisible reality.'

Janaka's face showed comprehension. How simple it all sounded! Ashtavakra then stated, 'Once you know the truth of your nature, as an enlightened king, your job will be to empower others with the knowledge that you have acquired. The kingdom of Mithila needs it now.'

'How do I do that? They are in the grip of extreme fear!' Janaka asked.

'Yes. For them, the approaching army is the reality. The army has been created from the fear they have.'

'O Ashtavakra! They think that I am being irresponsible. As we sit here, I am being condemned by my own people, my own court, my own family,' said Janaka.

'If you realize the truth, how can the praise or blame of others affect you?'

'I don't want Mahadev and the army to act out of fear. I would rather they act responsibly, in a time of fear.'

'Respected King, this is where you can make a difference. You have peace around you, because that's what comes from within you. They don't have peace, because that's what comes from within them.'

Janaka paused, as he struggled to assimilate all his understanding, 'I can see everything clearly. I understand the solutions for many of our problems. But what I envisage may be different from what others want, as their vision is clouded by the panic they feel.'

'So, what they see comes from them. But now, what you see should be the reality of Mithila. That's how you will become a responsible king, a true Videha. There's only a thin difference between you and the things around you. You are connected to everything and peace is in your inherent nature. This knowledge will liberate you.'

'How do you explain that?' Janaka asked.

'I will give you the classic example of the rope and the

snake. In ignorance, a rope may appear to be a snake. But by knowing that it is a rope, the snake disappears. If you are in darkness and somebody shouts, "Look! There is a snake" your first instinct would be to run away. You may feel afraid. You would pick up a stick to kill the snake. But then, imagine somebody else brings a lamp and lights up the area. You realize that it is not a snake, but just a length of rope. In the darkness, you mistook the rope for a snake. The moment you see the rope as a rope, the sticks fall from your hand and a new world of peace opens for you. The snake was only a projection of your mind.'

For a while, the two men grew quiet. Janaka absorbed all that the sage had said, feeling the truth in his words. But he wanted to know more, so he lifted his gaze to Ashtavakra, wordlessly urging him to go on.

Ashtavakra went on, 'Waves, foam and bubbles arise from water,' he said, pausing. 'And they disappear back into water in the end.'

Janaka could find no words. He nodded in silence. He was surprised to realize that Ashtavakra had told him nothing he did not already know.

The Conflict

Urmila, the king's younger daughter, ran to the queen's chamber and threw the door open. She rushed to her mother's side, gasping, as she told Sunayana and Chandrabhaga, 'There has been news. They say that Uncle Kushadwaja is on his way back. He's already near the palace!'

Chandrabhaga was overwhelmed with joy, hopeful that the news meant the end of all the chaos within the palace. Her spirit showed a merriment that had become increasingly unusual these days. She began to prepare herself with utmost care so as to honour his return.

Upon Kushadwaja's arrival at the gate, Sunayana hurried out with a salver full of tiny lamps, a coconut broken into two halves, vermilion powder and sandalwood paste. She offered Kushadwaja the blessings of a long life with the customary welcoming aarti, circling the salver with its flickering lamps around his person. She then anointed his forehead with fragrant sandalwood and auspicious vermilion. A sister-in-law, she believed, was more than a sister. She had prayed sincerely for his well-being regardless of what others had said. Before entering the palace, his feet were washed with pure, clean water from gold-plated pots.

Chandrabhaga longed to ask him of his travels and to urge him to relax and regain his energy. But before she had time to truly lavish him with her affections, one of the king's messengers burst into the chamber.

'My Lord Kushadwaja,' he said, 'The king requests an audience with you at once.'

Kushadwaja nodded, gestured to Sunayana that he would be back, and followed the messenger out the door.

❋

Janaka was not alone in the king's chamber. Mahosadha stood behind him, his gaze stern and unreadable, as Kushadwaja entered the room. The brothers locked gazes, and neither of them spoke for a long while. The look they exchanged was full of all the words they wanted to say but couldn't. But even in that shared silence, Kushadwaja seemed struggling to convey to his brother where he had been, why he had gone and what he hoped to accomplish now that he was back. Janaka nodded, and Kushadwaja lowered his eyes. They spoke the language of brothers, not of kings.

Finally, when this silent conversation had reached its end, Kushadwaja spoke. 'By the time I reached the Sadarina river, I found nobody there, but I could see the remnants of their stay. They had burnt their lodges and left.' He grew quiet once more, lowering his eyes to anxiously scan the floor.

A deep silence followed this statement, during which Janaka looked at the carved devas on the tops of the pillars.

Mahosadha gave the king a strange look, his face growing red. He fixed his gaze on Janaka, seeking or demanding answers from his king. Janaka seemed not to notice, or at least pretended not to.

'I have something else to tell you,' Kushadwaja said softly, casting a furtive look at Mahosadha.

'What is that?' Janaka asked, his voice steady and patient, but curious.

'Can we discuss this in private?' Kushadwaja asked quietly.

'If it has anything to do with the security of this kingdom, you can discuss it in the presence of Mahosadha.'

Kushadwaja started talking, hesitantly. 'I know that the enemy is advancing to the palace through a different route. My spies say that there were signs they had camped on that route. We took a short route to the Sadarina river as we were on horseback.' He paused for a while and continued. 'But now I must tell you something really serious.'

Janaka nodded in silence, waiting to hear the next words.

'I know that some people in the palace may already have this information.' Kushadwaja continued keeping his eyes fixed on the floor.

Mahosadha looked to the king, motionlessly waiting his response. His body was taut with tension.

'Have you not noticed? See, how he does not even have a reply? What does that mean? I have been telling you over and over again!' Kushadwaja's voice rose.

Mahosadha moved then, shifting his weight restlessly back and forth from one foot to the next. A moment later, he turned on his heel and strode out of the room without a word.

Kushadwaja curled his fingers, clutching at his robes, clenching them with his fists. Janaka nodded his head, but his expression was blank. He said softly, 'I don't think anybody within our palace is assisting Sudhanvan's men with information.'

'But did not you see Mahosadha's reaction? Why did he leave so abruptly?'

'I am not sure,' Janaka said. 'I will speak to him later.'

Kushadwaja's face grew pale, an angry glint hardening his gaze as he looked around the room, his jaw clenched tightly. Grasping his sword firmly with his right hand, he spoke tersely.

'There is only one thing for me to do.'

Janaka interrupted, 'No, you don't have to do anything about this. I told you, brother, I will find out about it later.'

The rage simmering in Kushadwaja's heart boiled to the surface, stiffening his lips into a straight, unbending line, giving new energy to his feet. He spun on the ball of his foot and left the room, every bit as silent as Mahosadha had been.

✣

The next morning, the king called for Mahosadha. The messenger returned and told him, 'Mahosadha is not in his quarters. Indeed, he has not been seen anywhere in the palace.'

Shock overwhelmed the king. He had not expected Mahosadha to hold a grudge over what had happened yesterday. He had, in fact, expected him to return much sooner. Even so, Janaka trusted Mahosadha and tried to put his adviser's absence aside as he went through the day's duties, and with his discussions with Ashtavakra. As the day wore on, unease settled in and Janaka found himself growing increasingly concerned. He did not want to believe that Mahosadha had gone somewhere without keeping him informed. Had something happened to his prime minister? He sent people to search the palace and the nearby quarters. They returned one by one bearing the same news: Mahosadha could not be found. By evening when there was no sign of him, Janaka began to pace.

When the door to his chamber opened suddenly, Janaka's heart leapt with hope. He whirled around to face the visitor. Relief surged through him. Of course, he hadn't been wrong about his most trusted adviser!

But it was Kushadwaja, not Mahosadha, who stood in the doorway, and his brow was furrowed in anger and concern.

'Mahosadha has not returned,' he fumed, his voice tense with barely suppressed anger. 'He has left the palace and told no one where he was going, or why. Brother! I have told you several times before that Mahosadha would cheat us, and now, he has done exactly that. He has packed his luggage and disappeared from the palace.'

Janaka nodded, carefully responding, 'I don't think Mahosadha would deceive us. He definitely has something to say. But he is unable to tell me for some reason that I cannot discern. I believe he has left the palace because the secret he is carrying has become a burden.' Janaka wanted to believe his own words, but he found himself faltering.

Kushadwaja frowned. 'This is what I don't understand. Even when you have the strongest evidence against him, you still trust him. Yet, you never want to trust me,' he said, his voice rising and growing stronger with his conviction.

'What kind of evidence are you talking about?' Janaka asked, confused.

'His sudden absence is the biggest evidence. Why is he not here to explain himself?'

Janaka did not reply, and Kushadwaja drew momentum from his silence. 'If he was not cheating, then why did not he tell you before he left?'

'That's what we have to find out.'

'Brother, it's very disappointing that Mahosadha has left the palace during our hour of need.'

Janaka blinked a few times, gathering his thoughts through his own confusion. He did not have an answer for Kushadwaja. For a moment, he was lost somewhere, but after some time, he pulled himself back to the present.

Forgetting for a moment that Janaka was his brother and

the king of Mithila, Kushadwaja's tone grew arrogant with unchecked pride. 'If you are not preparing to protect your palace against the invaders, then I am going to do what I have to do. Mahosadha, who should have taken this responsibility, has already left the palace. We need to act.'

Janaka frowned, wishing the rage in his brother's heart would lessen. Just as fear can cloud judgement, so can anger.

'And I have more important news for you,' Kushadwaja added, a moment later.

Janaka's frown deepened. 'What is the news?'

'Sudhanvan and his army must have already crossed the Daranya Mountain. They will reach Mithila in three or four days.'

Confession

Janaka summoned Kushadwaja early the next day. Kushadwaja rushed to the chamber, wondering if his brother had reconsidered his earlier ambivalence over Mahosadha's role in the betrayal. When he pushed the door open, his breath nearly choked him, shock lurching in his chest. Whatever he thought he'd find this morning, what he saw before him was not it. Inside, six guards wearing equally dumfounded expressions loomed over a man who appeared to be kneeling. Looking closer, Kushadwaja saw that both of the man's arms were chained behind his back. His legs were also shackled. The man's expression was unreadable. It was Mahosadha.

Janaka was staring out the window when Kushadwaja entered. He turned when his brother entered. Another ripple of surprise caught him unawares. The king's face sagged with uncustomary weariness, and tears trickled down his face leaving behind moist trails.

'Kushadwaja! It took some time for me to understand,' Janaka said, swallowing thickly, a deep sadness making his eyes droop.

Janaka gestured for the guards to leave the chamber. They silently obliged. Now only Janaka, the speechless Kushadwaja, and the restrained Mahosadha were left inside the chamber. Silence prevailed for some time, except for the occasional jangling of Mahosadha's chains as he shifted uncomfortably.

Finally, Janaka turned towards Mahosadha. 'You need to tell us everything that you know. We understand that Sudhanvan is on his way to Mithila. We have no time to waste, and we need to prepare to save Mithila and its people. We want to know what damage you have already inflicted. This is your chance to speak up. If you tell us everything, I will spare your life at least, but you will spend the rest of your life in the dungeon.'

Mahosadha looked at Janaka, his features smooth, untouched by worry or regret. It was in stark contrast to Janaka, who appeared withered with guilt, his shoulders slumping as he met his former trusted adviser's gaze.

'My Lord, I accept everything.'

Kushadwaja interjected, 'Were you behind all the plans, including the failure of the swayamvar?'

'Yes. I was.' He spoke bluntly, no hint of regret or guilt evident in his tone.

'Why did you do this? I trusted you more than I did my brother. I made open all the secrets of the palace to you. Did I hide anything from you ever? I always thought you were a man of principles.'

'I understand, my Lord! But let me explain.' Mahosadha paused for a moment and then said, 'I had a deal with Sudhanvan.'

'What was the deal?'

'I would help Sudhanvan conquer Mithila, and he would get Sita and the divine bow.'

'And what would you get in return?'

'He would make me the governor of Mithila with all the powers at my command.'

He paused to check Janaka's face for a reaction. Then he continued, 'I know that Sudhanvan is very powerful. But he is also foolish enough that I can easily influence him.'

'But Mahosadha! We have shared many things, and you have been part of our family. Why did you betray me? Did you not feel any concern for the people of Mithila at least?'

'O Lord. I am worried about the people of Mithila. It is they, I wish to protect. I understand that you cannot be changed. You are obsessed with a trivial dream, this absurd concept of enlightenment and going to the forest.'

Janaka stared at him, unable to comprehend how he had failed to notice that one of his dearest friends had not been aligned to his way of thinking. 'If you had such concern for our people, why, you could have spoken to Kushadwaja!'

Mahosadha did not flinch. But he nodded before speaking. 'Kushadwaja is not mature enough to handle royal affairs. Your son, Bhanumat, who you sent the sages into the forest, might just grow up to be exactly like you. So I took the responsibility of preserving the kingdom and its people into my own hands.'

'And betrayal then became your only option?' Janaka asked, sadness washing over him as he watched his cherished friend confess everything.

'I had only one way to do it,' Mahosadha said. 'I had to remove the thorn stuck in the flesh, with another thorn. I thought about it for many days and nights, and I weighed various options. I wanted to come and talk to you many times. But each time, you were immersed in discussions with sages. You were living a life far removed from reality. I thought about it. What should I do? Should I secure the kingdom or secure the king? Then I had my answers. Securing the safety of the people of Mithila was easier than transforming you.'

Janaka asked him, 'I nurtured you and loved you dearly. Where did I go wrong?'

'My Lord! I am your much-loved Mahosadha. I feel for you,

as much as you love me. But when your unrealistic thinking took over, I had no option but to do what I did.' He paused. 'You were wrong to believe that peace is the answer to your kingdom. Nowhere in history has peace worked. War is actually for the sake of peace, and not the other way around. War is required, to show one's power over others, so that people obey rules and don't indulge in violence. Negotiation can then take place and governance will become smooth. I had no confidence that you would accept what I would suggest. So I had no other way except taking my own course of action.'

Janaka felt a weight on him. His shoulders sagged further as he let out a weary sigh. 'But you invited our very enemy in. How could that protect Mithila?'

Seemingly untouched by his king's sorrow, Mahosadha went on, 'If I had listened to you, and if we were not prepared to protect ourselves against Sudhanvan, he would have attacked Mithila anyway. He would split this kingdom into pieces, and the people would suffer. You did not heed to the constant request to prepare for war. So I thought I would protect them by sacrificing the bow and Sita. Nevertheless, I did not think it to be any of your concern, since you already displayed an inclination to retire to the forest.'

Kushadwaja gripped his sword tighter and shouted at Mahosadha furiously, 'What did you do exactly?'

Janaka raised his hands signalling to him to lower his voice. 'Kushadwaja, he will tell us everything.'

Mahosadha continued, 'I formed a closed group within the palace to work for me. We blocked all the messengers from sending the invitations for the swayamvar. I wanted people to feel insecure about you as the ruler. I also wanted to make room for Sudhanvan to secure his interests. I had spies within the palace working for me. Remember, the security of the palace rests with me. So I could easily get things done. I had spies watching all of you. I had also influenced one of the sages to create an aura of fear, hoping that you would respond to the call for action. I tried to frighten Sunayana...' He paused.

'How did you plan all of this and who are the others?' Janaka asked, incredulously.

'I travelled outside the kingdom many times on the pretext of monitoring the threat from neighbouring kingdoms. It created opportunities for me to meet Sudhanvan and broker a deal. If it was not for your brother's meddling, everything would have gone as planned.'

'What do you mean?'

'I asked one of my spies to influence Kushadwaja to go to the Sadarina river, so that I could eliminate him.'

Kushadwaja stated angrily, 'So it was your men who tried to kill me?'

'Yes.'

Janaka was shocked. He started pacing the room.

'Do you have anything more to say?'

'I have nothing more to say,' Mahosadha's replied, looking down.

Janaka beckoned Kushadwaja to him. 'Put him in solitary confinement for the time being. Hunt down those who supported him. We will decide the rest of the matter in a few days.'

The next morning, the people in the palace woke up to grim news. Tataka and Subahu, the demons of the Bhayanak Van, the Forest of Fear, had been killed.

The king's messengers had rushed into the palace at dawn.

It was clear that they had ridden all night, so anxious were they to tell the king what they believed to be wonderful news. But it did not take long for the initial excitement to fade. The king was shut up in his chamber with Ashtavakra. He was unavailable for an audience. The news could not be passed to him.

The palace was agog. It was an unusal situation. It took only one thoughtful insight, one whispered rumour of fear, and suddenly the people of the palace were unable to rejoice over the demons' demise. While they were certainly glad that Tataka and her son were dead at last, they could not ignore the implication that the demons had been decimated by someone stronger than them.

Anyone with the strength and the numbers to take down Tataka and Subahu surely posed a serious threat to Mithila! If this feat had been accomplished by Sudhanvan and his forces, it must mean that they had a very strong army indeed.

The sky around the palace grew dark, as clouds formed. They shrouded the sun and hung heavy over the kingdom with the portent of rain. But the skies did not clear, and the rain did not fall. The clouds grew darker and closer, but the promised threat did not come to fruition. The king's sages were gathered outside his chamber, waiting for Janaka to come out. They chanted mantras and prayers for protection from any calamities that might fall upon the palace and the people of Mithila. Their faces were bowed, darkened by fear and trepidation.

The guards and soldiers were restless at their posts, pacing and talking nervously to one another, their focus distracted by the imminent doom coming their way. None of them had been able to sleep the night before, haunted by frightful dreams of war. If Sudhanvan's army was on its way to Mithila, they would be arriving in two days' time, right at the gates of the palace.

The Seed and the Plant

Meanwhile on the other side of the palace, Janaka, as usual, was closeted with Ashtavakra, disregarding the prevailing unease.

As Mahosadha was not present to issue commands to Senapati Mahadev, Kushadwaja took charge. But the army chief was waiting to get the order from Janaka, for without it, he could do nothing. As the afternoon drew close, Janaka continued to remain inside the chamber. The palace grew increasingly restless, but the chamber's doors remained firmly closed.

'Ashtavakra, the people of the palace believed I am wasting my valuable time with you. I know, they all believe that I have more important things to do than having discussions with you when we have news that affects the kingdom's security.'

Janaka paused for a while, collecting his thoughts, and continued. 'It looks like they don't have much hope, except for their belief that the magical bow will save them from the possible attack.'

Ashtavakra said, 'That's very good. Let them believe, because they need something to pin their hopes on. That's how people in general are. They want to believe in something, and that belief will give them enough power to sustain their existence. Men cannot live without hope. They usually find it somewhere. The collective mind of Mithila believes that the bow will help them, and this belief is good for them.'

'But does the bow have magical powers to thwart the enemies?'

'It doesn't matter, Maharaj. As long as they strongly believe in something, they derive strength and hope from it,' Ashtavakra replied, patiently.

'But it has to be true, doesn't it, to work?'

'O Maharaj. As long as they can draw strength and security in what they believe, it is right for them. So the question of whether the bow has power is irrelevant.'

Janaka tilted his head enquiringly and looked at Ashtavakra.

'I will tell you the story of a guru and a disciple...Once there was a disciple who kept asking his guru to reveal to him the secret of floating on water. When the request from the disciple became repetitive and annoying, the guru gave the disciple a mantra. He told him that the mantra would help him float in water. Thrilled, the disciple scampered away from the guru as if he'd received his life's biggest gift.

'Many days later, when the guru was crossing a wide river in a boat, he saw his disciple floating on the water comfortably. He was very surprised and called out to the disciple, who shouted back with elation to the guru, "I have practised your mantra and now I can float on water for hours on end."

'The guru replied, "I was just playing with you. What I gave you was not the right mantra. Be careful—you may just sink and die."

'When the disciple heard this, his feelings plunged from elation to disappointment, and in no time he sank in the water.'

Janaka listened, intent on the story and the wisdom he knew it would provide.

Ashtavakra continued, 'Whether the bow has any power inherent within it or not, is not the question. The power is in you. The reality of the bow, itself, is a delusion of the mind. If you believe there is power in the bow, you are consciously accepting that belief and it becomes a reality for you. You are consciously or unconsciously creating a *sankalpa*, and as long as it is from the source, the pure awareness, it works for you.'

Janaka shook his head, still confused. He drew his brows together questioningly as he looked at Ashtavakra.

'My Lord! As I told you before, your inherent nature is powerful and omnipotent. You can consciously create any belief you want and accept such a belief, and it will work for you. The most complex problems in the universe, which *you* think of as complex, can be resolved in the simplest way. The fact is, you are not aware that it is simple, and your mind makes it complex. You are not aware that you have been bestowed with the means that can create solutions. You have the key in your hand, but because you do not have the belief, you will break the door and enter.'

'Please tell me more about *sankalpas*, and how I can make them.'

Ashtavakra nodded.

'You are always making *sankalpas*, concisously or unconsciously, and you experience the results in your life. *Sankalpa* is the intention of something, something that you strongly wish for or look to happening. It is the one pointed declaration of a resolution made in one statement, in the present moment. When you want something, you have to think of it often enough, repeat the idea or the thought in a positive manner, so as to transform your life. This thought or *sankalpa* will harness your will, and the entire universe will work for you to achieve what you are seeking. This is the secret of all creation and the rule of all rules. *Sankalpa* is the intention that precedes all actions. It is the essence of our existence.'

Janaka continued to stare at Ashtavakra in silence, willing him to go on.

Ashtavakra continued, 'The foam and waves that arise from the sea emerge the same way a bracelet comes from gold. When you have this ultimate wisdom, you create your world around you from the thoughts you consciously create.'

At once, a question came to Janaka's mind. He asked, 'If we can create realities, then why are there chaos and problems in the world? Why can't we create only good things?'

'That's an interesting question. For your own consciousness and the universe itself, there is no good or bad, right or wrong. Whatever you create from your consciousness, they become real to you. A new universe arises from your consciousness. Your life is a continuous process of creation. When you make *sankalpas*, all the co-operative components of the universe align to bring forth what you really want in your life. You may not be consciously aware of it, but you can observe what you experience. If something contrary happens, you can create new *sankalpas*, so that new manifestations fold along your way. Become conscious of it, and you will enjoy this game. You will realize that what you have done till today is trivial compared to what you are going to do tomorrow.' He paused to look at Janaka.

'At the same time, there is also darkness in the universe. If you consciously create chaos and problems within you, you will experience the same. *Sankalpa* can work for you or against you, depending on your intent. This is what we have in all of our scriptures and the Upanishads, a process we enact during *homa* and yagna, the divine invocations.

'*Sankalpa* makes you decisive, wholehearted and certain. It is mentioned in the Rig Veda. It is the *sankalpa* shakti, the power of the divine, the will that creates the marvels of the world.

'Because you are powerful enough with infinite possibilities, let not your thoughts cloud you and stop you from tapping into the true potential you have within you. You need to be mindless and tap into your source, the ever-powerful, the non-physical you.'

Janaka nodded, enthused by all that he had learned. 'How do I know if I have made a *sankalpa* and that it will work for me?'

'You will know because you will feel it in your emotions. You will have the right vibrations within you. Soon after you created the *sankalpa*, you will have manifestations that will lead you to the right solution. Manifestations will unfold in the form of impulses, hunches, or something or somebody that will appear before you. You just need to know it, believe in it, and pursue it. Just like the seed sown by the farmer spouts and grows into a tree, *sankalpas* grow into realities around you. New life experiences will unfold. This is a secret game of the universe.'

'But Ashtavakra, there is something else I want to ask you. What if I create a *sankalpa* and it works against the *sankalpas* of other people? Which one will work then?' It was a thought that deeply vexed Janaka, because he wanted the best for the people of Mithila. He did not wish to harm them through his actions.

'Certainty of the belief determines the reality of a creation. Doubt arises when a vow is blocked by opposing views made by others or yourself in the past. When vows come from true awareness, from the source, life is originated and reality is effortlessly unfolded. This is how you become a true Videha, the bodiless, the one who transcends. You are not within your body, and you are beyond your mind, and beyond everything that surrounds you.'

Ashtavakra continued, 'You are the king of Mithila. That means the entire kingdom revolves around you. Your true leadership lies in how well you tap into yourself, witnessing consciousness and creating the *sankalpa* that provides the solution for your domain, which is nothing but your kingdom, the people of Mithila, and their welfare. Once you align yourself with the right *sankalpa*, your true nature has the power to overpower the influence of any other belief that arises from the collective mind. If the power of your consciousness is more powerful than the collective consciousness, you will thwart the problems they have the potential to create.' He paused and continued, 'The whole palace fears that the enemy will come. But if the belief in your domain, your *sankalpa*, is more powerful than their fears, you will attract the reality that you want to create.'

Fear

By afternoon, all the priests, the sages—Satananda, Seneka, Pukkusa, Devinda—and Senapati Mahadev were gathered in the assembly hall. From the oldest to the youngest, every single face reflected fear and hopelessness.

'This is the king's fault,' one of the younger priests whispered in a voice just loud enough to be heard across the room. 'If he hadn't been spending so much time with that sage, we would have had enough time to mobilize our forces!'

The man next to him agreed. 'I will not argue with the importance of learning. But if the enemy comes to our palace and carries Sita and the bow away, what good will the king's personal enlightenment do?'

'It is a matter of balance,' Pukkusa said. 'Even as sages, we see the importance of living a balanced life. Too much time spent on such matters is just as bad as too little!'

'Perhaps,' Satananda cautioned. 'But it is entirely possible that the king has a plan. He was warned of the impending conflict, after all, and...'

'Yes!' A red-faced man with a protruding belly stood up and bellowed the word. 'He was warned, and he chose to ignore the warning! What kind of a king is he? We must pull him out of that chamber and back to reality!'

The others murmured their approval.

'Who will speak to him, though?' asked Seneka. 'He has

not given us sages an audience thus far. It is likely that an intrusion into his discussion will be met with anger.'

'Send Senapati Mahadev!' one of the soldiers cried.

'No. He will not listen to a soldier! Send a sage!'

The argument raged until Satananda at last stood. The room fell silent under his gaze.

'I will speak to the king,' he said. 'It was, perhaps, my prophecy that brought this whole situation about. If he would listen to anyone in this matter, I hope that he will listen to me.'

With great trepidation, Satananda left the room and walked down the hallway. Behind him, the sages and priests followed, shuffling along in silence as he led the way to the king's chambers. He stood near the door, attempting to quell his own fear as he prepared to knock. There was no other choice. Someone had to get the king's attention, and the kingdom needed it now. It was time, at last, to interfere, or else the whole of Mithila would be burnt to ashes tomorrow. The king hadn't even heard the news of what had happened in Bhayanak Van, that Tataka and Subahu had been killed, and that whoever had killed them would surely be approaching the kingdom of Mithila.

Satananda lifted his fist and knocked. There was no response to his first set of knocks. But considering the urgency of the situation, Satananda knocked once again, and then he waited for some time. He stroked his long beard with his right hand, and while doing so, he glanced behind his shoulder a bit uncertainly. Was he taking the right action? All standing behind him nodded, assuring him that his motivations were sound. Satananda's courage was boosted, and he was about to knock on the door again, when it opened with a creaking sound.

Janaka stood framed in the doorway. For a moment, he looked at the people before him.

Satananda spoke first, bowing his head as he addressed the king. 'O my Lord! War is imminent. Sudhanvan and his army are close.'

Satananda hesitated, but continued his entreaty. 'My Lord! And just this morning, we have received one more piece of news. Tataka and Subahu were killed in Bhayanak Van.'

Janaka's brow lifted, his eyes widening with happiness, and he glanced around at his sages. 'That's very good news,' he said, 'And I think we should celebrate it. Tataka has been terrorizing all the sages and commoners for many decades. We have failed to contain her and her vile son. If she is dead, I see nothing but good tidings for the people of Mithila.'

Satananda looked around at his fellows. They exchanged glances, silent messages passing between them. Satananda stood uncomfortably, his shoulders slumped as he hung his head, unsure of how to express himself, despairing for the kingdom's future.

After some moments of uncertain silence, Pukkusa broke the quiet. 'We all assume that they were killed by the enemy who is approaching us, which means that the enemy must be very powerful. We need to be prepared as well. Their next move may very well be against us.'

'My dear sages! Why are you interpreting this wonderful news that way? If they have, in fact, killed Tataka, they could be our friends. As I have told you before, you are constantly living in fear, feeling threatened by thoughts of your own creation. Have faith in me. I promise you that I have not abandoned the people of Mithila. There is nothing to worry about. Those who have killed the demons have done so with the right intention.

It is nothing but good for Mithila. Don't you agree?'

Everyone fell silent. They did not know how to convince their king of the threat and the need to prepare for the probable war. Pukkusa continued hesitantly. 'Yes. But...my Lord! We all believe that an attack is imminent. We don't know how to convince you of this. Mahosadha is not around anymore. What we all request is that, in Mahosadha's absence, you assign the responsibility to Kushadwaja or Senapati Mahadev.'

Janaka remained quiet, listening with an expression of calm confidence. Perhaps it was intended to soothe his visitors, but his indifference only agitated Satananda further.

'O my Lord! There are many reports of an army of people approaching us from the direction of the Daranya Mountain. And the omens are very bad!'

Janaka did not react. He just kept gazing at them silently.

Satananda continued. 'O Lord! People have heard about this and have started coming to the palace.' Satananda gestured outside the window, drawing Janaka's attention to the courtyard.

The Nandivandana Courtyard was teeming with hundreds of people. More seemed to be streaming in. Their faces were grim, darkened by fear. The very silence of the people as they pushed their way forward was louder than any thunder, and just as ominous.

Janaka did not reply. He stared at the sages, his eyes clear, and his face devoid of fear. Then he spoke, 'Dear Satananda, fear has become your tool of control. A sage such as you, who I look to for advice, needs to have a bigger heart, an enlightened vision. Why, there is one among you, who is guilty of treachery. But you, Satandanda, I have always respected and revered you for your learning. I would wish my regard to remain. Therefore, leave me alone for some time.'

Satananda stepped back, shocked. He had not expected this. As he turned his head this way and that way to look at his fellow sages, the guilty one bowed his head in shame.

Outside, the sun was beginning to sink below the edge of the horizon, and the last of its rays were fading from the darkening earth. Night was falling. There were more than two thousand people, who had made the long trek from all corners of the city, muttering to one another. Their faces were fearful and their eyes darkened, their fear driving them to the palace of their ruler. Everyone knew that if the rumours were true, an unprepared Mithila would be unable to hold her own against the invaders.

The Veil

The night was darker than usual. It became heavier and more dreadful under the weight of the uncertainty of the people. Many of them had left the Nandivandana Courtyard, but a few hundred remained through the night. Morning filled the city with mist, and the people in the courtyard appeared like grey, ghostly figures. Nothing could be seen clearly, and the environs beyond the palace lay shrouded, as if in premonition of what was to come.

There were occasional commotions created by one or two, who panicked and screamed. Sages and brahmins were reciting mantras, praying to protect the palace from the impending calamity. The giant doors to the palace were drawn and fastened shut, the sound of their closing boomed like thunderclaps. As the reverberating echoes faded away, guards stood ready near the giant gongs, prepared for the call to battle.

In the morning hours, all of a sudden, the sounds of trumpets were heard from a distance and pandemonium broke out in the palace. Surely, it was the enemy army's warning, inviting King Janaka for war! Inside the palace, women and children scurried around, rushing to secure their own quarters and prepare what stores of food they could. Soldiers and guards ran around frantically inside the palace. Without any orders from their king, they lacked all sense of purpose in the wake of their fear.

At last the mist cleared, pushed away like a curtain by the morning sunlight. The scene beyond the palace became visible. A large army with elephants, camels, horsemen and foot soldiers with spears pointing to the sky, was silhouetted against the dim morning light. Smoke rose around the figures, curling and billowing in the air like a dark giant rising up with a fiendish look.

In perfect formation, the advancing army moved towards the palace, like a thicket of forest stirred to life in the misty morning. One of the horsemen from the group galloped ahead, towards the palace. Kushadwaja and Senapati Mahadev were waiting at the palace gates. The horseman was fearless, and it was a fearless ride—the optimism and confidence of the troops reflected in the horse's confident gallop and the bearing of its rider. Reaching the gates, the horseman removed his helmet and dismounted.

He bowed with respect to Senapati Mahadev and said, 'Dasharatha, king of Kosala has come to meet the king of Mithila. He has brought his sons Rama and Laxmana and the great sage, Vishwamitra as well. Rama is here to attempt stringing the divine bow.'

So stunned was Senapati Mahadev that at first he could not speak. Beside him, Kushadwaja let out a gasp.

'You…you are…?' the commander stammered, but soon collected his wits and returned the messenger's bow.

Kushadwaja couldn't hold back anymore. 'So who killed Tataka and Subahu?'

'They were killed by Rama and Laxmana. The princes, with their preceptor Sage Vishwamitra, went ahead of the troop and fulfilled the mission. We heard from the nearby village that the swayamvar has been announced by King Janaka.'

There was a murmur from the townspeople standing nearest to them. Soon the news flew across the crowd, in a smooth wave, the doomed expressions on the faces of the people changing to smiles. Mahadev rushed up to the balcony to deliver the news to the king.

There was a jubilant smile on Janaka's face as he listened. It was exactly as Ashtavakra had said about the snake and the rope. Thanks to fear, in the darkness of the mind, they had all imagined the worst. The blinkers had fallen now. He was at peace. He understood.

He ordered Seneka to organize a reception at once.

The huge brass drums on either side of the gate were soon pounding out a rhythm, and the waves of the sound reverberated within the palace walls. Joining the drum, a flourish of trumpets broke out. The citizens of Mithila laughed with the joyous sound.

The procession with King Dasharatha and his royal troops continued moving towards the palace. Soon, all the courtyards of the palace were teeming with chariots, elephants and horsemen. Flags marked in different colours, sporting varied signs were unfurled in the courtyards and from the balconies. A majestic elephant lumbered in, the royal pennant aloft atop the decorated golden chair on its back.

Janaka looked down at the scene from his balcony. Dasharatha, the king of Kosala, sat in the golden chair. His son Rama, with the radiant face, and his younger sons—Laxmana, Bharat and Shatrughna—ranged behind him. Hundreds of men, including the king's guards, and in the front, Maharshi Vishwamitra and scores of others, formed their escort.

A train of messengers, sages and ministers streamed the courtyard to receive the guests with the greatest honours. Girls carrying silver salvers with tiny flickering lamps arranged atop them, marked the foreheads of the guests with red vermilion powder in a gesture of welcome. Young boys and girls scattered flowers before them, while the sages and the chief priest, Satananda, led the king and his sons through the flower-strewn path.

The procession moved slowly, until at last it arrived at the courtyard before the palace. The two guards who flanked the giant gate lowered their spears and stood aside as Dasharatha and his sons approached. Janaka and all the members of his court stood smiling widely, palms joined in welcome, joy evident on their faces. Baskets of garlands were ranged by the gate, and resplendent young girls garlanded the visitors one by one as they walked by. The guests were showered with fragrant rose water, and offered sandalwood past and sweetmeats as they entered.

Janaka welcomed Dasharatha with due honours, and led him through to the palace hall, lit by dozens of lamps wedged into the pillars and wall. After offering seats to Dasharatha and his sons and bathing their feet with scented water, the girls looked at Rama's radiant face. Incense spiralled into the air, lending the occasion an aura of auspiciousness. The guests were given *arghya,* a drink made of milk and honey, and unbroken barleycorns to snack upon.

Kushadwaja took Rama and his brothers for a tour of the palace and showed them the royal gardens, meticulously laid out and adorned by rows of fruit-bearing trees. The servant girls came to Rama again, with hot water and fragrant oils for his bath, and fresh clothes and ornaments for him to wear. As they walked, silver anklets tinkled on their feet, and their hips swayed in time to the tinkling of the anklet bells. But Rama could only look at them with respect. The girls, sensing Rama's detachment, stole closer for a better look at the mysterious glint in his eyes. They became even more attracted when they realized their gesture of affections had no effect at all on Rama.

Meanwhile, Janaka, his face clear, his eyes sparkling, attended to the guests, ensuring that they were given comfortable rooms to rest, and were attended to by the palace staff. He looked around him. Flower garlands festooned every space; perfumes wafted in the air and laughter abounded.

Was this the same Mithila of a few hours ago? Was this the same palace that had seemed like a demon in disguise, waiting to pounce on him?

It was like a veil had lifted.

Illusions

Kushadwaja hurriedly entered the chamber where Dasharatha, Janaka and Vishwamitra sat.

'Oh, Brother! I have news regarding Sudhanvan.'

Janaka rose quickly from his seat and asked Kushadwaja, 'What is it?'

'Sudhanvan has fled back to his kingdom. He did not cross the Daranya Mountain. When they were camping at the foot of the mountain, Sudhanvan received news that King Dasharatha and his sons were in the vicinity. He also heard that Tataka and Subahu had been killed and that the demon clans had been vanquished. When he heard that Dasharatha was heading towards Mithila, he fled. He understood that these two kingdoms aligned, meant he had no chance of a victory if he attacked.'

'Inform everyone of this news. It is a great moment in the history of Mithila. Give orders to organize the swayamvar immediately,' Janaka declared.

❊

It was like a dream.

The entire kingdom of Mithila fell into a great celebration once again. It was the biggest that had ever happened in the history of Videha, or any other Arya kingdom. All the festivities that had been put on hold were revived, and the Nandivandana

Courtyard was again filled with thousands of people celebrating the occasion.

The sages had their confabulations and fixed the day for the swayamvar. Entertainers stood at ready on the streets and the palace courtyards. The people of Mithila had many reasons to believe that the swayamvar would be successful and that Sita's wedding would take place soon.

Festivities and entertainment were aplenty. The roads of the city were washed and cleaned, and different types of banners were hoisted on either side of the road. People celebrated by beating drums and dancing. The tantalizing smells of a variety of cuisines started wafting from the palace kitchen. Giant gongs were struck, conches were blown at intervals and waves of joyous sound passed through the streets of Mithila.

As the news spread, kings and princes from the neighbouring kingdoms made their way into Mithila, to be accorded a grand welcome. Janaka was busy receiving the guests with all due courtesies.

Sunayana was beaming with happiness. She rushed around, receiving ladies of the high dignitaries. She looked brighter than she had for the longest time, in her golden sari studded with rubies and pearls. Her heart was finally at peace, especially upon hearing from the king that their son Bhanumat was ready to come home from the gurukul.

The hall where the bow was kept was bedecked again for the swayamvar. The bow lay on a silk sheet, covered with fragrant flowers and incense curling up into the air.

Soon, the day arrived. There was much excitement as Sita was once again decked as a bride, her sister and cousins accompanying her to the hall. The kings arrived one by one, and were led to their seats by members of the royal family and courtiers.

Once the gathering had settled down, Janaka got up, and with Sunayana, offered prayers to the bow, showering flowers on it. All the people gathered in the hall stood up as well, palms joined in veneration and silent prayer.

Janaka announced loudly to the audience, 'Today, once again, we have here the bow and Sita in her wedding dress. Whoever can lift the bow, string it and release an arrow from it will be eligible for my beloved daughter's hand.'

Sita sat on the dais to the left side of the hall, dressed in bridal clothes decorated with diamonds and pearls from top to toe. Her delicate earrings tinkled as she moved. The light caught on the intricate jewels she wore, shining on the golden belt on her hips and the jangling bangles on her wrists. As usual, her sister, Urmila, and her cousins Srutakirti and Mandavi were also present.

Janaka bowed to Rama, inviting him to take the test. The young prince stepped towards the bow, softly touching it with adoration. He silently offered a prayer, his lips moving while chanting mantras. He then scanned the audience from left to right, bowing his head as if invoking their blessings. The watching crowd roared in jubilation. Rama glanced at Sage Vishwamitra and his father, Dasharatha with bowed head, requesting their blessings. Vishwamitra raised his right hand in blessing, while Dasharatha smiled and nodded. When the rumbling of the crowd reached a crescendo, Vishawamitra raised his hand and gestured for them to be silent. They quietened down and held their breath. Sita's heart throbbed. She closed her eyes in prayer.

Rama lifted the bow with his right hand and balanced it.

He held it upright, as he pulled the string from one end to the other. Just as he strung it, the bow snapped; the sound reverberating deafeningly across the hall. It was so loud that a few people in the front row fainted. As the echoes died down, the gathering exploded in cheers. Rama's eyes met Sita's for a dazzling moment, aglow with the enchantment of divine love.

In Sita's heart, a flower bloomed. The cosmic wheel of time changed its course to set a new direction. Mithila was getting ready to embark on a new journey.

Accompanied by her maids, Sita walked slowly towards Rama, a flower garland in her hands. Conches were blown in unison to mark the auspicious occasion. As she reached him, Rama bent so that she could place the garland on his neck.

King Janaka led Sita and Rama to the platform where the wedding ceremony would take place. The fire altar on the platform was lit, and the priests began chanting the ritual mantras. The ceremonies began, as the young couple, their upper garments knotted in symbolic fusion, circumambulated the fire seven times. Bells were rung, conches blown and music played. The joy on everyone's faces was a sight to behold.

When the ceremonies were over, the young couple sought the blessings of the elders at the assembly. Once they were done, Vishwamitra stood up and gestured with his hands for the audience to be silent.

'At this most joyous occasion, I have to make an announcement.'

The assembly paused, the silence attentive. 'Rama has three unmarried brothers who are here with us today. To further strengthen the unity of the kingdoms, I propose that the brothers of Rama marry the beautiful damsels of Mithila:

Mandavi, Urmila and Srutakirti.' The crowd roared in delighted approval.

✻

Janaka looked at the people around him, filled with joy and exultation. He pondered: *How happy they are! They think that it is an everlasting state of mind. The same people who were fearful and worried have suddenly become joyful again. What if another disturbance happens? Will they again be swayed like a pendulum?* When people are not in constant motion, they seem lost in a world of obliviousness, often intoxicated by their own folly or benumbed in lethargy. People are awakened only by sensual pleasure, fear, or threat, and then the mind again plays its cruel game of distracting them, taking them to different worlds. *What is everlasting joy for them? As soon as the merriments die down, people will find reasons to be unhappy.* When they have no problems, they will find ways to create them, and thus emerge conflicts, wars and other absurdities in life.

The king's jubilant expression faded and he grew pensive as he sensed a misalignment somewhere. Something bothered him. Was this moment meant to be celebrated? What is the state that does not change, that is everlasting? He remembered Ashtavakra then. His eyes searched the crowd, but the young sage was nowhere to be seen.

Epilogue

Like a leaf in the wind
the liberated one
is untethered from life—desireless, independent, free.
18.21 ASHTAVAKRA GITA

The celebrations continued. Janaka beckoned Kushadwaja to him. Kushadwaja bent to touch Janaka's feet, but the king held his shoulders with both his hands and looked at him intently for sometime.

'Kushadwaja, I know you have undergone a lot of hardships. I was blinded in so many matters. I couldn't distinguish the right people. I failed to recognize your intentions or support you when I should have.'

Bowing his head, Kushadwaja spoke, 'Oh, Brother! That's all right. Now that everything has ended well, you don't have to think about it much.'

Gesturing to Sunayana, who stood beside him, Janaka continued, 'Even Sunayana went through a difficult time. I owe a lot to both of you. But, Kushadwaja, we have still bigger things to worry about. Ravana is still at large, posing a threat to all of us.'

A guard entered the hall and quickly strode to the king. 'Maharaj, Sage Ashtavakra is at the gate. He seems troubled. He asks that you meet him at the gate.'

Surprised to hear this, Janaka started walking briskly towards the gate. He found Ashtavakra waiting there; his features stiff, distant and indifferent to all the celebrations.

Janaka spoke, 'Ashtavakra, today is one of the most important days in the history of Videha. Can I invite you to take part in the celebrations? Rajkumar Rama has broken the bow. My daughter Sita was married to Rama, fulfilling her destiny in what will be a positive change in the history of Mithila. We are embarking on a new journey. Don't you want to join us in the festivities?'

'Definitely, Maharaj! But, I have a request for you.' Ashtavakra's voice belied his smooth expression. It was choked with emotion and he could barely speak the words.

Janaka's eyes widened in surprise. Ashtavakra was never motivated by the material, and him asking a favour for himself, was a surprise in itself. He was overcome by curiosity.

'Of course, Ashtavakra! Ask whatever you desire.'

'Now that Mithila has overcome its challenges, the swayamvar has taken place, Tataka and Subahu are no more, and the demons have been vanquished from Bhayanak Van, can we recall the seven sages who you sent to the Himalayas?'

Janaka was taken aback. He stared at his young preceptor with new eyes, wondering how he knew of such a secret mission.

After a moment's pause, Ashtavakra swallowed and spoke again. 'Kahoda is my father. I have never met him. He came here before I was born.'

Janaka blinked. Whatever he had expected to hear, this certainly was not it.

'I am surprised, Ashtavakra,' he said. 'Once I heard that Tataka and Subahu were dead, I sent messengers to the Himalayas to inform them to finish their tapas and join us. They should already be on their way and will arrive here in a few weeks.'

The sudden roar of exultant cheers coming from the Nandivandana Courtyard interrupted their quiet but enlightening conversation. Janaka took the moment to look up at the sky, as fireworks burst in the darkness, creating an array of stars that created a divine glow all around them. When he looked back at Ashtavakra, he saw that the sage wore an intense expression of relief and joy. A smile now spread across his face. Meeting the king's gaze, he dipped forward in a bow of gratitude, and the king bowed to him in response.

'Ashtavakra! I have one more question to ask,' Janaka said.

Ashtavakra nodded, tilting his head curiously.

'This will probably be my last question,' Janaka said, smiling.

Ashtavakra nodded again, gesturing with his hand for the king to continue.

Hesitantly, Janaka spoke, 'Which is true? The dream world or the conscious world?'

Ashtavakra did not speak. He looked away, and then looked back, finally meeting the king's eyes with a slow smile.

'Both of them are untrue—the dream world and the conscious world.'

Janaka's face lifted in a smile that matched Ashtavakra's. He nodded and turned, waiting for Ashtavakra to follow him. Ashtavakra followed the king slowly with his distorted gait, placing his stick on the uneven ground to help him along. Janaka and the sage made their way back to the palace where his daughters, guests and his people were waiting.

Another wave of fireworks boomed and crackled amidst the night's festivities. A flourish of trumpets broke out in the background, sounding pure notes of celebration accompanied by the deep bellow of the conches. In response, the people roared their exultant joy.

Janaka slowed his pace for Ashtavakra, and he looked around him, at the atmosphere of tumultuous joy.

Is what I see real?